FINAL SOLUTION

FINAL SOLUTION

RICHARD E. PECK

Doubleday & Company, Inc., Garden City, New York
1973

ISBN: 0-385-08744-6
LIBRARY OF CONGRESS CATALOG CARD NUMBER 72–89340
COPYRIGHT © 1973 BY RICHARD E. PECK
ALL RIGHTS RESERVED
PRINTED IN THE UNITED STATES OF AMERICA
FIRST EDITION

for
Earl and Mary
and especially
Donna

FINAL SOLUTION

blackness

blackness droning

muted distant murmuring

tries to defend garbled cluttered syllables clashing on all sides strains to shut them out and learns volition

recognizes that the noises impinge on "him" he understands selfhood. And duration.

He waited an indeterminate time while the sounds rose and fell.

That's how Kiley will have come out of his coma. It will be confusing. Something like being born full-grown. Later, he will find that it had been painful. But the pain is not yet remembered at the point in time where we have joined him. Which is nice, for Kiley.

Feeling precedes thinking.

And not only for Kiley. No one infers a pending earthquake.

1

"Reform has been attempted before, to little effect. A challenge confronts us. Let us begin anew."

Preface, *The Kiley Proposal*

FLICKERING LIGHTS plucked at his eyelids, and he squinted against the intrusion. A wisp of dream faded into gray thirst. Discomfort shimmered in some faint memory. Not precisely pain, it was the implication of pain. Flatulence and heartburn. He tasted pennies at the back of his parched throat. The sensation faded as he felt his chest heaving, and a chill washed over his uncovered body. He tried to curl tightly in on himself, thought *blankets*, and strained pinioned arms in a futile attempt to cover his nakedness and delay waking.

Morning.

Erection.

All 61 university water systems are dosed with "antirect" 340 days a year. Antirect accomplishes what saltpeter was rumored to do. Several years earlier HEW had pretended blindness while Women's Lib guerrillas substituted antirect for fluorine in university drinking water. (Actually, CIA agents disguised as Women's Lib guerrillas [actually[2], FBI agents who had infiltrated the CIA].) The government therefore couldn't be blamed. It *had been done*, passive voice. No one in authority admitted responsibility.

For many of us it won't matter any longer. Not by then. We will still remember nonholiday erections. Even the morning spontaneous sort. People inside a university wouldn't believe that. Neither will our grandchildren. We won't care.

But for the adults in Kiley's audience—he will be posing in public—his flaunted manhood seemed coyly archaic, like nose rings worn by cute aborigine children seated at a missionary's feet (see any pretape issue of *National Geographic*).

The background noise swelled to a base cheer at the sight. Soprano hissing cut it short.

Kiley's eyes were not open.

An unseen speaker said, "Look'at mothah. He wavin hello."

"Sheet! He ain't nuthin but flinchin."

Third voice, feminine: "No. Bobby right. He comin around. We done it." Pause. "You think can the cameras see him?"

Rustle of cloth settling over his startled loins. Snickers.

"Hey, Jackie. Why you coverin him? You ain't 'barrassed?"

"Enough there!" A phlegmy bass growl. "I say this for the record. At oh-nine-fifty-one this date, subject appears to be awakening up, in accordance with our expectations elsewhere recorded. Subject's eyes are open."

Three suns loomed overhead. Clouded masses shifted and wavered between Kiley and the light. The moving forms leaked into one another like dancers in a smeared watercolor. He fought to raise a hand but found his arms strapped down.

That made his nose itch. So you see, some things won't have changed after all.

Unbidden tears welled up in his burning eyes and made him feel foolish. He wasn't crying. He couldn't help it. The facts of physiology are irrefutable, a case of matter over mind. Traces of water trickled slowly down his cheeks and into his ears.

Three ghostly pale, white-clad figures bent low over him. On his left stood a girl. Jackie. She clutched one end of a gauze sheet, which billowed like a sagging tent slowly collapsing across his groin. Beside her were two men grinning a welcome at him through translucent membranous masks, sweat beaded on their glistening white foreheads. The suns overhead backed into focus within silvered cones to become high-intensity lamps.

"Is this a hospital?" he will think he asked. It came out "Ahhrawaagh?"

One of the men laid a rubber-gloved hand on Kiley's bare chest. "You gon be okay, Mis' Kiley."

"Okay's ass," the other said. "Famous, is the word."

Before Kiley can repeat his banal question, which simple observation would have answered for him, the phlegmy voice recites: "Transfer to cryogenics recovery hereby authorized, oh-nine-fifty-four this date, as per schedule determined the fifth instant. Doctor Howard Bengston, Director Combined U-Fed Project one-sixty-two-slash-Kiley."

That's another thing that won't have changed. Dr. Bengston will frequently refer to himself in the third person, in phrases replete with title. Some people are like that. At breakfast he regularly reports to his wife, "I had a thought last night, dear. I said to myself, Doctor Bengston. . . ."

Kiley doesn't know that yet. He does know he is not fond of Bengston's gravelly voice.

"Now this is off from the record," Bengston said. "But I feel we can all congratulate ourself on a job well done. I don't feel we could of done it without the help of those individuals who all contributed so much to this project, and I'm confident you all know whom they are. Our success ought to prove one thing, I feel. We can work together, man and female, Fac and Bizad, young and old alike, irregardless of racecreedorcolor. There were some individuals who said that this that we have accomplished couldn't be—uh—accomplished like we have . . . done. But I feel. . . ."

The gurney on which Kiley lay began to clatter away from the guttural droning. The noise it made drowned out the noise Bengston made. Toward that end were square wheels primevally ordained for all hospital gurneys. If you wait long enough, everything makes sense.

Kiley passed out.

2

"Had lunch today with three special program kids [LAUNCH ("Likely Although Underachieving New Career Hopefuls")]. All seemed lost at [the] U. How [can one] get them settled in?"

The Notebooks of Robert Kiley
(as edited)

WHEN HE AWOKE there were more voices.

". . . like perfect. One of the gyno-obstets in the observe tiers done call it 'normal birth.' You don't have no worries with a boy who get hisself born that way, all his tools workin like. Why not the same thing, does a full-growed man get resurrect *homos erectus?* You just *knows* he gon be somethin special."

Kiley opened one eye carefully. The last time he had done that, Bengston had begun to orate, and Kiley didn't want to risk it again. Delirium often clouds our understanding of cause and effect.

The girl said, "The newshawks makin such a thing of it. They been carryin on like—"

"You ain't still listenin to them?"

Kiley couldn't see Bengston, and the pair in his room seemed to be ignoring him. He went exploring. He moved one tentative hand beneath the sheets and found the restraining straps gone. He had already guessed that. His nose didn't itch.

He opened the other eye and examined his surroundings. The bed he lay in was backed into the squared-off point of a room vaguely tetrahedronal in shape. That is, like the wind-direction indicator beside an airport runway.

Beyond the sheeted mound of his feet, at the base of the reclining pyramid that was his room, Jackie and a man stood looking away through a glass wall, their backs to him. The apex of the canted ceilings above them hung a full nine feet from the floor; at his end of the room—notice his tendency to become possessive—at his end of the room a scant foot separated his head from the juncture of white ceramic planes above. From an open panel in the canted ceiling, curved rigid tubing reached toward him and pressed a rubber pad against his exposed arm. As he jerked the arm away, he felt the snatching hiss of suction. Evaporation chilled his skin.

The pair at the window turned. The man was short, bulky. The woman glowed in the light; her pale complexion had the depth of fine china.

"He wakin up," she said. She depressed a stud in the ceiling/wall, and Kiley's bed lurched into motion to glide silently toward them. "Feelin better?"

He nodded and grabbed the mattress. The bed stopped.

"I'm Jackie Muller. This here T. T. Trotter, only he leavin. I'm spoze to help you get it together. Anything you want, I lay it on you. Dig?"

Kiley was puzzled by her diction. We may be too—at the moment—but we won't be when she begins to speak. That's over fifty years from now. Remember: they laughed at Demosthenes and his pebbles. And look how well he turned out. It's not for us to mock Miss Muller.

Kiley nodded. "Water?" His throat was stuffed with cotton.

Trotter grimaced. "How's that for quotable first words? He gon have to start puttin down somethin better when Bengston get here. That man got hisself ass-deep in Facreps and reporters all hot to go, and no more stallin, less we gives him some reasons. And Morgan want to know was the money wasted or not. I'll tell Bengston what shakin. You get Mis' Kiley set square fast as you can." He turned and walked into the canted wall/ceiling. It split to reveal a narrow V-shaped window in the corridor outside.

A stool rose from the floor beside Kiley's bed. The girl sat to meet it. She leaned forward and guided a flexible tube from the headboard to his mouth. Ice water. No more plastic pitchers and brackish sludge. Progress.

Kiley sucked in the cool water and lay back to wait. Too many questions buzzed through his bewilderment for him to single out any one of them.

"We was 'spectin some disorientation," she will say. "But you gotta start gettin it on your own self. I'm a cue ideas. You 'sociate. Mainly it's up to you."

For a moment Kiley said nothing. The water had helped. Whatever had earned him this hospital bed couldn't have been too serious. He felt fine—strong, well, "recovered"—and obviously as fit as he'd ever been: he caught himself automatically weighing and measuring the girl. His thoughts toyed with seduction, or with estimating the girl's potential as a seducible object. Consciously, he focused on her exterior. Subconsciously he thought about nerve endings and their stimulation. We know that by analogy to our own ogling.

He saw: five-foot-five (we still won't have adopted the metric system), 120 pounds, wrapped in translucent white; strapless slippers clinging to her stockingless feet; good legs, long, slender, crossed now; no bra, luminous-dyed nipples lifting behind pockets on the uniform; a single blue vein tracing its way up from neck to ear; no makeup visible on her face—which argued expert application of makeup; lips pressed tight in anticipation; nostrils flared a bit—too much for "beauty," but strong, somehow; eyes blue, bright, neutral; curling brown hair cut short and mannish. One glance back over surveyed territory made him erase the adjective. Mannish didn't fit.

"Any time you ready, if you seen all you interested in."

"Am I supposed to feel guilty now?" he asked, his face flushed with guilt.

He waited for an answer. That shows nerve.

"Let me start," she said.

He blushed. That shows lechery.

Flushing is pink; blushing is red. It's a matter of intensity. Emotional states are not ranked alphabetically. Language is not logic.

"One." She raised a schoolmarmish finger. "I'm Doctor Jacqueline Muller. Two, you in Room 14A, Temporary Cryogenics Wing, UU Labs Complex. But was I to go spillin more'n 'at, chances is you won't react straight up. So you tell *me*. What's the last memory you got?"

"You mean I've had amnesia?"

She flounced. A man might have sneered. There *are* differences.

"Try this. What do the name Paul Loris mean to you?"

"Paul? He and I. . . ." He remembered.

Now the story gets sticky. It might be argued that Paul Loris isn't yet (our time) involved in the way he will have been. And for him to see this account might change his involvement, make him behave differently. There isn't a real answer. Is predestination restricted to a Sunday season? As a possible solution to the problem, consider the number of people who read nothing, or those who read and never act on what they learn. Loris might be one of those.

Besides, if we boggle at every minor paradox, we'll never get the truth told.

Robert Kiley, then, and Paul Loris, and their celebration. It happened the day the Faculty Senate at Urban University voted to accept The Kiley Proposal. Kiley hadn't chosen that name, but the flattery implied wouldn't hurt his career. He welcomed any help, however accidental. A most junior instructor, with neither a Ph.D. nor any serious intention of getting one, Kiley considered himself lucky to be an afterthought on the committee charged with redesigning the university. They called themselves COPE ("Committee on Premium Education"). As junior man, Kiley did the legwork, running down facts and figures, interviewing students, gathering data. As junior man he drew the task of compiling and writing up suggestions based on the committee's deliberations. As junior man, he sat silent while others introduced and explained the proposal. Only at the end of an interminable Senate session, when faculty appetites voted to approve (it was well past the dinner hour), had the program been named: The Kiley Proposal. The phrase had a fine ring. Kiley left the auditorium on a cloud of applause.

Paul Loris, one of the few reactionaries who had voted against the proposal, swallowed his irritation and began to boast of his own recent work. They walked off together, both talking, neither listening. They ate a sandwich at The Paper Doll, both drinking too much in celebrating separate successes together. They walked through the spring night back to Loris' private lab, past the still smoldering burned-out shell of Prior Hall, past the armed guards patrolling the campus-ghetto interface at the newly established campus perimeter, past small groups of students muttering in the darkness.

In the basement lab, drinking Loris' concoctions of ethanol-and-whatever, their conversation drifted from Kiley's success to Loris' secret project. It was a running joke between them. In spite of their friendship, Kiley had never believed half of what he thought he understood about the whole matter: cryogenics; tissue cultures in liquid helium; something devious in Paul's diversion of government funds from approved research to personal use. Kiley had often tried to persuade Loris of the obvious risk to his career involved in a project so patently insane: Frankenstein was a loser. Loris always answered with waspish comments about semi-educated humanities instructors.

That night will have been different. Loris was elated and insisted upon proving his claims. The two men stared bleary-eyed through frosted-glass observation ports into refrigerated specimen drawers of various sizes. Inside each of the smaller drawers, a single organism floated alone—"isolated," in Loris' rehearsed pun—and waited to be awakened from chill sleep. Two large drawers were empty. On a stand at the end of the storeroom-become-laboratory, three foot-long carp swam golden and glistening in a large aquarium. The steady thrum of compressors forced the men to shout.

"Eight weeks," Loris said. "Frozen solid eight solid weeks, and there they are."

"Fine. That's just fine."

"Three out of ten, good as new."

"What about the other seven?"

"I never claimed it was perfect."

"Kind of tough on the fish who didn't make it."

Loris mounted a demonstration several uncounted drinks later. Earthworms lay under a glass bell, and invisible gas hissed through writhing rubber tubes into the bell, where the gas liquefied and dripped over the still worms. The glass frosted quickly and hid the worms from view.

While Loris tapped the glass gently and crooned to his pets, Kiley grew bored. The floor had developed an unnerving slant, and his teeth felt furry. With careful concentration he managed to lick his lips. He needed some air.

"Going outside," he shouted.

Loris hung onto the workbench with one hand and waved the other, too busy to be bothered.

When Kiley opened the lab door he heard a strange coughing sound. *Flat, flat, flat.* He climbed several shifting concrete steps and pushed open the outer door. The stench of acrid smoke greeted him.

Cautiously, he poked his head out into chaos. Billows of oily smoke belched from the shattered windows of West Hall, a distant siren keened and drew near, crouching silhouettes stuttered wildly across the mall toward cover, while that coughing sound repeated at random intervals. A sniper. Atop the library. Kiley saw the muzzle flash and watched one of the scampering silhouettes topple and lie like a heap of discarded laundry.

"Paul! Come on up! They're at it again!" he shouted down the stairwell toward the lab door. "Paul!"

With both hands braced against the wall, Loris climbed the steps in slow motion, grumbling unintelligibly. "Interrupting. Can't get a goddamn thing done in this place. What's the matter now?"

"Burning West Hall, I can see the fires. And there's a sniper out there."

Loris nodded his head silently for a long moment. "Right. Right. What did I say? Right. And that's the bunch you're going to cool down with your stupid proposal. That's not what they need. *I'll* tell you what they need."

He pushed past Kiley and stepped outside into the flickering, demonic light. "Knock it off!" he yelled. "What the hell's the matter with you?" He stood, arms raised, as if silencing the multitudes. "*I'll* tell you—"

Flat, flat.

"Paul! Get out of there!" Kiley lunged at Loris and missed, falling to his knees. A part of him sobered enough to recognize his own drunkenness; he willed each motion deliberately and seized Loris' leg. Rolling to one side, he dragged Loris down on top of him and lay panting.

"Inside," he said. "Back inside."

They crawled toward the fan of light marking the open door. As they reached it a rainbow burst in Kiley's eyes; his throat caught fire, and a gout of acid seared his lungs.

That sequence will be all Kiley remembers.

3

". . . until you come out of it today," Jackie finished for him. "We don't need no more specifics. We mostly knows about that part anyway. So you wing it, we fills in the gaps later." She pointed at a button-tipped rod jutting out from the side of her stool.

Kiley knew what it was without asking.

"Tape banks. No chance losing somethin before we gets time to analyze. The Facreps wants it for proof. Bizads is lookin to catch us short. But don't let that bug you none. There's been some changes you need to know about, without you let your enemies pull some shit on you, surpriselike."

He was puzzled. No one has claimed that Kiley was particularly quick. But you would think he'd have begun to put pieces together.

Instead, he lay there wishing he could blink his ears. He kept waiting for her to explain her jargon. If he had asked her, he might have precluded some later embarrassment. He always was too patient.

Jackie's eyes glazed and told him she had left the room. She pressed one hand to her ear. After a moment, she nodded. "If you thinks we should."

He knew her comments were directed elsewhere. He fought the impulse to scan the room for hidden visitors and instead watched her speak once more to the microphone at her side.

"He ain't really makin it as of yet. If you bring them in, I wants it understood you doin it against my advice." She shook her head and murmured inaudibly, then said to Kiley, "Some men wants to see you. It's three of them outside now, so get your head right. My advice is, don't say nuthin. No chance you pull a mole, without you don't say word one. They mostly wants to look you over, 'sall."

He watched the men enter.

First, carrying himself with all the authority of a bell captain, a man in his fifties waddled shimmering in an iridescent suit that shone like raw silk and whispered money. His silver hair lay cropped close to his skull, shorter than the shaggy white eyebrows that hovered above slitted, wary eyes. In spite of his reek of power, he walked like a man with a bulls-eye fastened to his back.

Behind him shuffled two men, one Caucasian, one black and wearing a multicolored dashiki. The black sported a jeweled comb in the crimped explosion of his hair. His companion concentrated on a small touch-button device, which he cradled in one hand and tapped with the other.

The leader produced a labored smile. "Well, now. Our patient seems fairly alert, wouldn't you say?" He glanced back to the men behind him and included them in his forced pleasantry.

Kiley recognized the rasping voice.

"I am Doctor Howard Bengston. These gentlemen are Barnes and Noble."

"*Doctor* Barnes, brother," the black said, extending his hand.

Kiley shook it, noticing Bengston's frown and Jackie's slight approving nod. "Bob Kiley, but I get the feeling you know that."

Barnes grinned. "If I don't, I ain't got no business bein here. When you think can you shake off them sheets and come talk to us? We been studyin on you long enough. Time is we was gettin to rap some. 'Specially before Brother Bengston here start tryin to convert you."

Bengston harrumphed his way toward a speech, but Jackie interrupted.

"You come in too quick on us, Doctor Barnes. We ain't but hardly got started. Let me give you a for-instance. Mis' Kiley? What would you say is today's date?"

Before he spoke, Kiley had the feeling he was going to be mistaken. Their accents, attitudes, even the room itself seemed wrong. He looked to them for a clue, but they maintained a stiff silence. Noble's hand had ceased its tattoo on the keyboard he carried. Barnes stood with his head cocked to one side.

"Well. Let's say mid-May. I can't tell how long I've been here, but the faculty meeting was May 9, so—"

"What meeting?" Barnes demanded of Bengston.

Bengston was still involved in the speech he had mentally organized but not delivered.

"Quiet," Jackie said. "No, Mis' Kiley. The year. What year is it?"

"Now dammit! This is getting silly. It's May something or other, 1973. If you—"

"You mean he don't know?" Barnes asked.

It was rather surprising. But in Kiley's fund of ignorance that small tidbit is scarcely worth noticing.

Jackie answered. "We can't just throw this shit at him like that. I mean, it's shock involved, you know? I ask that mothah Trotter to tell you. Why you think am I here? Mis' Kiley still don't know his hat from his ass, and you come bustin in figurin you suck around and get some one-up on the rest. Well, it doesn't work like—"

"It '*doesn't*,' sister?" Barnes' face froze, but his eyes blazed obvious anger.

" 'Scuse me," Jackie muttered. "I didn't mean nuthin."

"Now, doctors," Bengston interrupted. "This is a group effort. I feel we must maintain—"

"Fuck-off, Howie-baby," Barnes snapped. "I don't need no fade bitch layin her white mouth on me. If he don't know, time he did. Now dig it, Charlie. Today is November 15, 2024."

Kiley closed his eyes and smiled. It had to be something like that. Either the whole crowd of them were raving, wall-climbing maniacs, or he was. At that moment, he will not feel like giving odds.

But don't be smug about his mistake. We tend to think in the same linear fashion as Kiley. Otherwise, why do we have verb tenses?

4

"We are confident that the several colleges and departments within the University will accommodate their respective differences under a major plan pointed toward achieving the good of all. We must eschew divisiveness."

Preface, *The Kiley Proposal*

HE WILL WATCH the four argue briefly, and almost inaudibly, near the door. Only the name "Morgan" came through to him— several times, in tones of fear and reverence. The specific content of their disagreement isn't important. Kiley could infer the battle lines.

Barnes' anger melted to petulance as he bowed to Bengston's chin-bobbing adamance. Then they left.

Bengston stalked out, Noble immediately behind him still tinkering with the device he carried, and Barnes a sulking figure trailing them unhappily.

Jackie remained. Her grim look dissuaded Kiley from asking any questions.

He had enough to ponder as it was. First, he was no longer strapped down. His legs burned strangely, but he could move, and that was an improvement. Though no one had used the word "prisoner," Kiley felt like one. He debated several plans for getting free.

He was practical enough to decide that escape was unlikely. He couldn't get far in the nude. His explorations under the sheet told him that the hospital hadn't issued him a gown. His only immediate inspiration came from an old Errol Flynn movie, in which Flynn had overpowered his guard for the uniform.

His twenty-third appraisal of Jackie's form suggested flaws in that plan.

He nevertheless wasted two minutes considering the attempt. When it grew clear that his glands were dictating suggestions, he resorted to reason. The whole charade intrigued him. His bewildering predicament might be dangerous, for all he knew. Still, he had always enjoyed puzzles, though he had never solved many. In this case—why would anyone want to kidnap him? He had nothing anyone might want. No family except his father, a grocer and part-time dowser in Vineville, Illinois. No money worth counting. Neither enemies angry enough to want him harmed nor friends imaginative enough to rig such a complex practical joke. It was inexplicable.

He considered himself a fairly simple, uncomplicated man. We all do, but he was right. When he completed his annual insurance renewal forms he wrote "teacher" rather than "professor." He had more or less average tastes in music, food, women. Call him a minor-grade intellectual with pretensions to practicality.

He had few vices. They were unimpressive on any familiar scale.

Virtues? Equally undistinguished. But one stood out in his mind. He knew himself to be patient.

We would call it laziness.

He either decided to wait and see, or he failed to decide anything. It depends on your point of view.

The girl seemed content to wait as long as he. She stood near the window with her arms folded across her chest, and the back light hid her face. Kiley couldn't evaluate her expression. He found consolation in trying to outstare her. And he resolved to regard his situation as an adventure. They were rare enough in his life. He applied the old axiom: if rape is inevitable, relax and enjoy it.

She gave in first.

"Want to start over?" she asked. "Try and forget what you seen and hear just now. They shouldn't come bustin in like they done. And they ain't bug us no more till we gets you on your feet."

She flustered. "'Scuse me. I didn't mean nuthin."

He waved a magnanimous hand. It is easy to forgive what you don't understand.

"Maybe it's time you was grittin some solids. Then we gon talk." She crossed to his bed and depressed a button on the headboard.

The button would ring a buzzer that would alert an orderly, who would bring a meal. It was most efficient.

"Don't let Doctor Bengston shake you none," she continued. "He be a good head, for a Bizad, just tryin to pull off somethin ain't nobody think he can."

"Who was the quiet one? Noble?"

"Doctor Noble? He like Bengston's secretary. It figure Bengston, he shook somethin might happen to the tapes, so he makin sure he got a record of what go down here. Noble, his job to take notes. Maybe he gon write up some reports."

"That makes Bengston a somebody, to have a Ph.D. for a secretary. Or is Noble an M.D.?"

She looked puzzled for a moment. "My mole, looks like. But try and remember, it's hard for me to know what's cloudy to you, same as you ain't dig what's my straight up. Noble a place to start gettin it on.

"First, from the way you talkin, must be you had some secretaries without no doctorate or nuthin. But Noble, he can read and write, probably got shorthand too. Wouldn't even surprise me none could he use one them old typin machines. So Noble ain't your ordinary tape secretary or hypnorecaller. A real Ph.D. Probably even read your books, like I done."

His glazed look defined his confusion. He admired her knack for changing the subject without seeming to realize that she'd done so. But he misunderstood; he had merely missed the steps in her logic.

"My books? Okay. Now it's all starting to make sense. You've got the wrong Robert Kiley. Is that it? Do you think I—"

"Don't come shuckin me," she blurted. She breathed deeply, like someone pantomiming hard-won patience to an obstinate child.

"I'm a try best as I can, but I don't need no contrariness to screw me up. You think is this easy for me? Bengston ain't want no Fac here anyway, 'specially no woman. But I went intensive for three solid weeks when I hear they set to bring you out. I read your books three, four times, and I mean *read*. Them old paper-and-type versions. If it's anyone know you better'n me, I don't know where they at. So just cut the jive."

Kiley's feet had fallen asleep. Ants nibbled their way along his shins. That tended to distract him. Still, he recognized how serious she seemed, and he didn't enjoy having her angry with him. He wanted to be loved. Like the legendary palm trees, he bent before the wind. "All right then. What did you think of my—uh—books?"

"Now you figurin to humor me, is that it? Listen. I knows things even you done forgot. Want to hear? Like the car you stole in high school, that your old man cover it up for you? Or the Kramer girl, she blame some stupid mothah for her pregnancy just to save your chicken ass? Or about—"

"Drop it." He let himself sink into the cushioned mattress. He felt weaker, and his legs throbbed painfully. "How did you—"

"'at don't signify none. I *knows* you, man. And that why Bengston have to let me have this job. But also I know how many people it was spend their time hidin your mistakes. You ain't catch me on that same limb. Did somebody else come around and replace me, how fast you think could they clear up your head? Some cat come in here cold, you start shinin around and keepin yourself safe out of trouble. But that shit ain't work on me. So it's just us, till I say different. Dig?"

Kiley grew more embarrassed than puzzled. She did know him, in ways he didn't enjoy knowing himself. We all have secrets. She had uncovered a few of his. He felt more naked under the sheets than he had moments before. She knew which buttons to push to make him react; and that's knowing too much.

Suddenly she looked dowdy. Familiarity is more effective than saltpeter. You can't seduce a girl who knows you have holes in your socks. He pulled the sheet higher and shrugged.

Jackie seemed calmer, more relaxed. She accepted his unvoiced submission. "Right on. Now I'm a hope we wouldn't have to do it this way, but Bengston want you told. Doctor Haller, the new UU prez, he got you set for some public meetings in a few days. Maybe Bengston right.

"Truth is, Mis' Kiley, you a puzzle to me. I don't know how could a bright man be so slow about stuff. So one of two things. Either you playin dumbhead 'cause you figure to snow me for reasons I ain't dig, else you ain't really what we been hearin about so long." She stared at him as if seeking a reaction. "Or either the doctors is right, one, and your memory shot. But when Haller let the newshawks get at you, you damn well ain't gon fuck up the Kiley everyone think you is."

She flipped something at him sidearm, and

5

he caught it in self-defense. It was a letter from Paul Loris.

Dear Bob,

This is about the hundredth draft of a letter I'm not positive you will ever see. The other ninety-nine didn't satisfy me, neither will this one. But it has to be written. If you're reading it you probably won't need any explanation besides what you've already been told, still, I have to try.

When those maniacs shot you I wasn't in much shape to think straight. I'm beginning to think that was all for the best. I got you into the lab alright but your neck and shoulder looked like they were all torn to hell. The phone didn't work either. At the time all I could think was try to keep you safe till I could get a doctor in. In the morning it didn't seem like such a good idea. There you were in the big drawer you called my morgue, and I was scared to death about trying to bring you out again.

Since then I've had twelve years of the most insane luck imaginable, just keeping the secret. My problem, and your problem too, has cost me three other jobs away from this asylum because I didn't dare leave Urban and let someone else into my lab. Sooner or later they will find out what I did. All I can do in the meantime is keep working and try to patch some of the holes in my ignorance. You're "safe" as far as I can tell, although so many problems remain unresolved that I'm less confident now than ever. I'm still working with the carp, up to six out of ten now.

I've kept a pretty good log of my work. Several researchers out in the real world and away from this jungle are working too, with approval and real funding. They've already published the results of research I might have done, if I hadn't been involved with you. That's not really a complaint, for all I know you saved my life, but the last few years I haven't felt like thanking you for that, either. I won't bore your incompetence by describing the research I mean. The technical details wouldn't mean anything to you anyway.

In one way you were lucky. Your wound didn't look too bad after the bleeding stopped. Freezing was almost instantaneous, it's that "almost" that worries me. Cell damage of one sort or other is certain because of mechanical rupture through crystal formation and differing cellular osmotic rates. As yet I have no solution for that difficulty, and the problems of dehydration are even more complex. A man at Hopkins is doing good things with dehydration, if I could only get away from here to see his work firsthand. Now that travel is forbidden, I couldn't leave even if I wanted to. I'll have to settle for the published results.

All I can tell you is that I've devoted my life to working out the best recovery process. One way or another, whether you get to read this or not, the effort won't be wasted. Although I don't imagine that fact would satisfy you.

It won't satisfy me either, I do have a conscience. Try to picture my panic the next morning, I had to conceal what I'd done. Later I was able to rationalize my cowardice by telling myself that "confessing" wouldn't bring you back. Only I could do that, and only if I had my freedom. By the time the newspapers finished speculating about your disappearance matters were settled for me.

You were a nine-day wonder. *The Kiley Proposal* was published by the University Press and every nitwit in the country bought a copy. Then some of your bleeding-heart colleagues ransacked your office and collected all the notes and scraps they could. They edited what they call *The Notebooks of Robert Kiley* and issued it as a sequel. Now people discuss you in hushed tones and Capital Letters as if you had been canonized.

They never did catch the sniper. They don't even connect you with him. Current speculation sees you martyred by some insane classicist or—worse yet—by a "mad scientist" irritated at the shift in University policies liable to follow our adoption of *The Kiley Proposal*.

So now I spend my time praying I can accomplish something before funds are cut off completely and I'm reduced to teaching grad students how to light a Bunsen burner. I pray to my own efforts, though, and maybe to you, because like it or not you're both my punishment and my exoneration. It's your turn to repay me. By reading this letter you'll be guaranteeing that people will eventually forget *The Kiley Proposal* and recall instead the genius of,

> Your frightened friend,
> [signed]   Paul Loris

It was a lot to absorb at first reading. But it rang true—Loris' petulance muting the intended apology. The letter answered questions Kiley might not have thought to ask and surprised him very little. He had sensed the truth since Barnes' verbal explosion. Now he understood it.

"Rip Van Winkle," he muttered.

Given time, he might have chosen a better analogy. Loris' carp, for instance.

"Okay." He waved the letter at Jackie with one hand, kneading his aching calves with the other. "I see some of it. But you'll have to explain better than you've been doing up to now. No more of your double-talk."

He flipped back the sheet and swung his legs over the side of the bed. Jackie lunged to restrain him, too late. The dizziness that swept over him couldn't blank out the sight of two cumbersome, translucent blocks dangling from his ankles. In place of feet.

His legs disobeyed him and he lurched forward into the girl. His face caromed off the soft flesh of her thighs and crunched to the floor, where sparkling lights blossomed behind his eyes. Before he blacked out he heard his own distant voice: "Now I probably broke my goddamned nose."

6

KILEY's first few hours of resurrection will prove unpleasant to him. The alternative would have been less appealing. Asleep for thirty-four years under Loris' protective eye, for another seventeen exhibited to scientists visiting the university on a federal pass, he had been content. He didn't know what went on "outside" his peace, any more than we will know what transpires "inside." His sleep was not unpleasant; and no one enjoys that Monday-morning alarm clock.

The blocks replacing his feet gave him no discomfort, though he was not fond of staring at them. Neither did he appreciate the image reflected in the mirror that Jackie reluctantly brought him:

a shirt would cover most of the scars cross-hatching his neck and shoulder, but he assumed that a man totally hairless—no eyebrows or lashes, nothing to comb, no reason to shave—might attract attention in the public streets. Something about glandular imbalance, they told him. Irreparable. Even that shock he endured with equanimity.

No single problem, physical or emotional, was severe enough to make him wish Loris' experiment a failure. He will assume a petulant stoicism.

And all these fainting spells will pass. He is really a well-conditioned young man, not given to physical frailty. Handball twice a week, long walks in the park with girls reluctant to see his apartment—that sort of thing.

It is convenient, however, to mark off episodes in his new life by concluding them where in fact they end; that is, as he loses consciousness or control of a situation. Those concern us most: his consciousness, however limited it might be; his control, however seldom he might exercise it.

Yet the world does go on, with or without Kiley in conscious attendance. He had cast his bread upon the waters, and the ripples are still spreading.

7

"The University must recognize a moral obligation tacitly accepted with each student admitted. In a time of narrowing employment opportunities, each University should undertake to hire its own products. It would thus benefit from the superior experience theretofore afforded those products."

The Kiley Proposal

"Business School has a guy [Professor] teaching Insurance! Where the hell did he come from?"

The Notebooks of Robert Kiley
(as edited)

ETHEL PEASE dislikes her late shift in the Department of Electronic Security. She seldom gets home before midnight; and in order to see her son eat breakfast she must rise by six, take the subway two miles to the Department of Child Care, and stand outside the one-way window. If only she had thought to get that man's name, she might have persuaded him to marry her. She knew that any of several men might have been Warren's father. Still, it was the big one she thought most about. Married to him, she would have been able to keep Warren with her, rather than sending him to Child Care to be raised Warren Urban.

It was an old lament. All of Ethel Pease's laments are old, familiar, habituated. In the human brain there lies the potential for millions of synapses to be actuated. All it takes is the movement of an idea, the minor electrical impulse along a single neuron, a simple jolt of chemical stimulation, to form a memory. With each repetition, that memory becomes stronger. But, unstimulated, the brain remains a virgin plot, waiting for a chemical reaction that never comes, waiting for that spark of current. The brain of Ethel Pease was nearly static-free and powerless. Only a few repeated ideas sputtered along its pulsing surface. Among them was her nightly lament over not having got, that, man's, name.

Each night, sitting here listening to the forcefield shell cracking outside her office, she sighed over the same collection of ifs. It never did any good. Perhaps she knew that. But her idle time filled itself, and her mind worked with the only material it had stored.

The bell rang to interrupt her reverie. Actually, her reverie ceased a nanosecond before the bell sounded, as it did every twenty minutes, every night, out of habit, but she did not know that. The bell rang to mark her interrupted reverie, and she sighed as she climbed out of her chair.

Time to check the equipment again. Lately, students had begun to experiment more cleverly with shorting out the field. They threw wire mesh against it, or buckets of water, anything they thought might break the curtain of flickering green power that domed Urban University and reached to the ground here at Exit East. Now, almost nightly, they gathered nearby to taunt Ethel Pease, and she had grown too fat of late to chase them away.

She climbed the grillwork steps to the platform overlooking the control panel. Six dials to read, in order, left to right. On each dial face a needle pointed toward a colored arc on the perimeter of the dial. Green, green, yellow, yellow, gray . . . red. She checked the dots tattooed on her wrist, although she knew them by heart: green, green, yellow, yellow, gray, gray. Something wrong with No. 6.

She plodded to the end of the platform, to No. 6 rheostat, and seized the big wheel with both hands. She turned it slowly, carefully, until No. 6 needle moved into the gray; then she paused to listen.

Perhaps she heard a change in the field, perhaps not. It still crackled outside, and above, and around her station. Now all the needles pointed where they should.

She clumped back down the grillwork steps, sighing. How did people get so old so fast? Every time she made this particular descent she pondered the same question; its frequent recurrence had something to do with the effect of gravity on her brain. Nearly forty, came the thought. All her girlish plans, long since abandoned. She had wanted to go on to graduate school, but something had gone wrong. Twenty-eight years ago—that wasn't her calculation; she thought "once"—she had been among the first to take Retardo. It hadn't worked so well then, or perhaps it hadn't worked on someone eleven years old. In either case, it hadn't worked completely. During her senior year, after eight faithful years on Retardo, her breasts had begun to develop.

She took to skipping her hygiene class with that nice Professor Floy. Why take the pill? It wasn't doing its office. And then she grew proud of her sprouting pubic hair, and the swelling visible under her blouse.

Some of the men noticed. She knew the stories. The first few months off Retardo were always the most difficult, the body crashing through years of puberty in mere weeks, but none of that had mattered. Men noticed. How could a young girl, completely inexperienced, fend off all the men during holiday parties? That big one, especially. She could still picture him. Well, not picture him. But she could remember what he had said; that she could do. A Full Professor he had been, something to do with machinery, or tools, or the Foundry Department—it was all so long ago.

As her hand touched the tea kettle handle, another synapse closed. Warren. Warren had been born. The nice doctors in the Department of . . . wherever it was they delivered the babies, those doctors had done something inside Ethel Pease, as they did to all unmarried mothers, and then there would be no more babies. With no husband, she had no chance of moving out of the dorms.

Off Retardo, she had no chance of entering graduate school. Luckily she had finished her B.S.—belly corseted, armpits shaved— in time. She knew her colors and numbers. They could trust her. Of course she would not make trouble, not with Warren where she could see him through the one-way glass three times a week. Of course she wouldn't risk her faculty status by letting someone sweet-talk his way out Exit East.

Ethel Pease was faithful to her charge. No one left Exit East without proper authorization tapes. She kept students away from the controls and away from the field itself. And she never missed a day.

With a totally subaudible hiss, Ethel Pease's train of thought switched tracks. She unfolded her newspaper. It was that time of night. All four pages contained pictures. Under some of the pictures there were printed legends, but the Department of Electronic Security forbade Ethel to have a trivee set in her office, so she could not hear those legends read on the late news. She looked at the pictures on page one: one, two, three, four, five, six, seven—seven wrecked cars. Seven accidents since yesterday. At the bottom of the page a basketball team hoisted its coach high overhead; in the adjoining frame, a group of dejected basketball players sat slumped on a bench. After a moment's thought, she picked out the winning team.

As she opened the paper to the center two pages, a small card fell to the floor. On it was a drawing of a reclining man whose penis stood erect, incredibly out of proportion.

"Pssssh!" she said. "Some kid drew that."

Next to the reclining man stood two students, holding hands. One might have been a boy, one a girl. It was hard to tell. They were both students.

Idly, she turned the card over. On the back, several words were printed in block capitals. She squinted at them for a moment, but letters always gave her a headache. She dropped the card into the office wastebasket and took the whistling tea kettle off the burner. She would have time for a cup of tea before the bell rang again and made her check the dials. Green, green, yellow, yellow, gray, gray.

One thousand disproportionate sketches of Robert Kiley were distributed with the evening newspapers. Most were overlooked, ignored, discarded. Sixteen were saved by students who sensed a disturbing comment in the contrasting figures sketched on the card. Five were actually read.

All within the few minutes before Ethel Pease sighed and climbed the grillwork steps to check the dials once more.

8

"As adults, our students have the right to choose the fields of study most fruitful to their interests. Only in the rarest of circumstances should any collegial body presume to dictate courses of study to those persons most affected in the educational process—the students themselves."

The Kiley Proposal

THE NEXT few days of Kiley's then-consciousness were filled with detail, much of it not relevant to the new life he was preparing to live. He is interested in relevance.

He learned, for instance, that all rooms in the hospital were

shaped like his. Between each pair of tetrahedronal cells there existed
a matching shape, inverted, in which were stored the several hospital life-support systems, testing apparatus, food supplies, medica-
ments, and linens. It made him feel like a bee in a hive.

A drone.

He did nothing but absorb.

Jackie told him who he was, or was thought to be. It was a les-
son in historiography. Time had made of him a hero. The Father
of the University, they called him. The Man Who Made Education
Relevant. The titles were endless and impressive.

Kiley was most impressed, in a proud, humble way.

Until they let him read his books.

"I'm not going to understand a thing you say, if you stick to
this slang you're using," he complained to Jackie.

"Page one hundred sixty-four," she intoned. Her eyes rolled back
into her head as if seeking the reference there. She handed him an
opened copy of *The Kiley Proposal*.

"A major hindrance for the minority student is his inability
adequately to communicate in standard English. Current attempts
to change his speech patterns are predicated on assumptions
which attack his very life-style and seem to effect little change in the
student, except for making him feel even more the outsider than
his condition actually warrants. One way to alleviate this problem
might be to institute classes in the dialects of minority English, for
students to whom such are the familiar and habitual language patterns (see Appendix J)."

He recalled the paragraph perfectly. To his mind, he had written
it only a week earlier.

He did not recall the footnote: "As this book goes to press, the
Urban University Department of Humanities is preparing to offer a
required class in black English, based upon current usage patterns
indigenous to the surrounding black community (see Appendix K)."

"What's that mean, 'required'? For *all* students?"

Jackie nodded. "Ain't that obvious in what you say there? How
you think does somebody feel when the rest of their class talk dif-

ferent? So they done like you said. Now it ain't nobody gon feel put down no more." She waved a hand over the university sprawling beneath the balcony of Kiley's hospital room.

Through the smog he could see no more than a few blocks of the eighty-eight square miles of campus. Still, the sight added to his sense of well-being. He was, somehow, "Father" of all that.

"You don't mean Puerto Rican kids and whites, do you?"

"No favorites, no more," Jackie catechized with obvious pride.

The idea would take some getting used to. It might even make sense. Other questions had begun to answer themselves for him. In the past few days he had grown accustomed to the clattering racket his prosthetic clogs made on the tile floor. The throbbing was gone from his healing nose. Except for his total baldness, and a few minor scars, he felt the same man he had been before his death, fifty-one years earlier.

He drew assurance from all sides. Jackie hovered over him like a mother hen and ministered to all the needs he had courage enough to describe to her. The medics assured him that the technician who had broken off Kiley's feet when moving him from the helium tank had been reprimanded. Accidents like that were minor, considering the major miracle of their having revivified him at all. They also promised that brain damage had been slight and reversible. With much tact, they said, "You'll begin to think clearly in a few days," suggesting in the process that the thoughts he now savored were less than brilliant.

"So if it's anything you ain't remember like they say about you, just tell them you done forgot. And if you pays attention, it ain't nobody gon mind little slips."

"Now, dammit! Knock off the dialect."

Jackie burst into tears and ran inside.

He debated following her but decided against it. He began to read. The orderly had brought him tapes, then shook his head in admiration when Kiley asked for the books themselves. The orderly had never seen anyone read, and he begged permission to watch, but Jackie chased him out.

She was afraid Kiley might begin to feel "different."

Kiley mentally toyed with the phrase "perish, *then* publish" as he hefted the bulky tome. Its very size was imposing: 300 pages— 54 of text, 190 of notes, 56 pages of bibliographical introduction.

The footnotes were even more intriguing. His short paragraph on the advantages of an open-admissions policy was followed by 6 pages of notes. The notes cited authorities he might have drawn on (3 pages), precedents for his suggestion (2 pages), and possible benefits accruing to any university that adopted what was called "Article One of *The Kiley Proposal*." Summarized: if everyone who applies is granted admission, no one is left out. That avoids invidious comparisons. If all who desire university degrees are awarded same, society benefits. And by opening wide the gates, university administrators might preclude trouble from those persons previously excluded for transparently unjust reasons under the discriminatory cover of admissions standards.

For which read, it should stop the burning.

He clomped inside, scarcely leaning on his cane. "I didn't mean it this way." He waved the book at Jackie.

She sniffed.

"Cut out the femininity. I know better. Now, are you here to help me or not?"

"Ain't I got feelins, too?"

"About as much as a crowbar. Don't forget: I watched you tie into Barnes, right in this room."

"Then you start criticisin the way I talk, like you some kind of expert or somethin."

"Okay. I give up. You do it good. There ain't nobody—"

"*It* ain't nobody."

"*It* ain't nobody does it better. But for Christ's sake can't you save it for someone else?"

She seemed mollified. In a moment only the streaks in her invisible makeup recalled her unhappiness.

"Can we talk about this alleged book of mine? I'm trying to tell you, it's not the way I wrote it."

She pantomimed exaggerated patience again. "Look, man. You gettin the. . . ." She hesitated at his glare, then shrugged. "All right. You're getting credit for the suggestions offered there, or for the way they're currently understood. What does the rest matter? We've already got enough opposition from the Bizads. They've been agitating for reading and writing classes again. If you contradict everything we've accomplished, you'll be playing right into their hands."

He decided to feel consoled. She assured him that fewer than 10 percent of their students could read. Almost no adults bothered to try. No one could misunderstand what he couldn't read; and distortions in the audiotape versions of *The Kiley Proposal* seemed far enough removed from Kiley's authorial hands that they didn't matter. He couldn't be blamed for them.

He was the new boy in school. Better to wait and see.

9

"Every group here [seems] determined to protect [its] own interests. [One] never saw such pigheadedness. Business School, Liberal Arts Faculty [a rare instance of Mr. Kiley's misunderstanding the evidence]—all of them [except Fac are] blind to any other point of view."

The Notebooks of Robert Kiley
(as edited)

WAITING has several advantages. He rests in the eye of a hurricane. Outside his serenity, forces circle and growl and contest for his attention—everyone wants Kiley's favor.

He passed pleasant days in constructing metaphors for all the activity he could infer but was prevented from seeing. Urban U. had become more confusing than he remembered—a melting pot over a cold burner, its contents susceptible of combination but uncombined. That will be his function. Kiley was resurrected to supply the heat.

From his window he saw security guards ringing the building. Jackie was kept busy with conversations he couldn't understand. He heard only her muted side of them as she spoke into a blank phone screen. But Kiley is a bright man; he began to recognize that his future was the bone of contention over which all the opposed university factions were fighting. He even came passively to understand some of the confusion swirling about him.

The Bizads are interested in training their students, in developing members of a managerial class, and methods be hanged. "Accountability" is their watchword; what are the results? What Kiley doesn't understand is their motive. Successful Bizads earn their way clear of the university forcefield shell, and thus "success" to Howard Bengston can mean the opportunity to drop his burden and never again to demean himself through contact with unwashed masses of adolescents. If Morgan comes to admire Bengston's achievements, Bengston can leave Urban U.

Part of this Kiley has inferred. The rest will come clear to him. For now, he is content to know that the Bizads want his help, for whatever reasons.

Facreps, too, want him. It's wonderful to be wanted, though already Kiley's popularity has begun to inflate his ego. Facreps want his approval for their having followed *The Kiley Proposal* to the letter. How can he deny them (without denying himself)? So far as he can tell, Fac are interested in their students' well-being, a laudable trait. What he does not know is that a Fac-trained student can never leave the university. If he knew, he might not care.

Everyone outside Kiley's hospital room is planning his future—that much he knows. It will save him the trouble. And, should they be "wrong," it won't be his fault.

He says now, and will say time and again, that he is not responsible.

But the buck has to stop somewhere. "Human nature" is the cop-out's answer.

For the moment, Kiley doesn't think. He enjoys.

10

"A valid objection is raised by many students. They lack control over the very administration which is intended to serve their needs. Reform in the constitution of the Board of Trustees and in the manner of selecting high-ranking administrators is sorely needed. We suggest. . . ."

The Kiley Proposal

PHILIP J. HALLER enjoys being president of Urban U. The hours are good, his duties are light. He will conduct periodic press conferences and supervise the vote counting for university referendums. He will draw his mark on the annual budget request, which Morgan prepares.

Even his detractors will agree that he was perfectly suited to his post. He had a loud voice. He could count to one hundred unaided, given enough time.

His election had surprised no one. He was the tallest man in the Department of Buildings and Grounds—six-foot-two—and every triveecast of a burning building showed him to good advantage. He became known. He was quoted, and his comments offended no one. No one understood him.

When Bizads and Fac foolishly nominated distinctively different candidates for the post vacated by the assassination of President Borgward, students spoke—in Haller's name. The entire electorate, all students under twenty-one, had a clear conception of the qualities needed by their president. Haller had them. He represented the perfect compromise. He was neuter (actually bisexual, but the imagency of Whipporwill, Wister, and Shanks got him a good press) and talkative without being communicative. He never had to alter an opinion; he had none.

He stood on the platform behind the bulletproof plastic body-shield and held both hands high overhead. Two fingers on each clenched fist were spread as Vs. It meant nothing. Advanced arthritis had made him a natural for politics. (By that time, we will have knotted knuckles, too. Six years from now the AMA will pressure Congress to make the sale of therapeutic copper bracelets unlawful. They never worked, anyway. Neither did the bracelets.)

In the auditorium, before Haller, sat one hundred observers, reporters, Fac, and students. Seventy-two blacks sat in their own section. After admitting and counting the blacks, Haller had instructed the general-at-arms to admit twenty-eight whites. He kept the percentages matched to those of the university population at large. If two rooms had been available, he would have admitted one hundred people to each.

While the crowd muttered, Haller counted the house. There were fifteen women, thirteen men. He had achieved the proper sexual balance as well. He didn't count black men and women; they all looked alike to him.

It was time to introduce the speakers. He could tell because his shoulders were tired.

"My fellow Americans [tired chuckles]. I spoze you're all wonderin why I ask you to come here today [one strained smile, from a Professor of Shoe Repair who had come in looking for a rest room and did wonder]. I want you all to meet Robert Kiley."

He looked at the chairs ranked behind him on the platform and searched a moment.

Kiley raised a hand.

The crowd cheered.

"Yes, him. The bald cat with the funny-lookin glass feet [appreciative laughter]. That's the one there. These others is here 'cause they like done somethin to bring Kiley out from the ice box where they was keepin him. Like Bengston there. He done the most of it, I hear."

Bengston preened and cleared his throat loudly. He had anticipated this moment. All morning he had rehearsed his address.

Haller continued.

Bengston sulked.

Kiley tuned Haller out and stared at the swamp of faces beyond the footlights. He imagined them as bits of noodle floating in a broth. Staring, he began to identify isolated features. A nose here, there an ear. It unnerved him.

When the applause told him the proceedings had reached a transition, he looked at Haller.

Haller was pointing his Vs at him.

Kiley took the cue and rose to clump forward. Treat them like another class, he told himself. Nothing to worry about.

"I don't have any prepared remarks, except to say that I'm glad to be here [snickers]. Right. I'm glad to be *anywhere* [applause]. But you all know more about that than I do. Why don't you ask the questions? I'll answer as well as I can."

He turned back to look at Jackie. She was seated at the end of the row of chairs behind him. She nodded approval.

The questions started.

For twenty minutes, matters went well. Many observers were curious about how Kiley had felt while unconscious, what sensations he could recall. He remembered nothing. Some questioners had historical queries, most of which he couldn't answer. One woman persisted in asking his opinion of certain "classic" television series, then refusing to believe that he couldn't remember them. All in all, a harmless session.

Until one man rose to ask, "Why is it you ain't talkin black?"

Scores of indrawn breaths left a vacuum in the room. The hush was tangible.

"Well, to tell you the truth, I never learned."

A gabble of voices swelled. People vied with one another in their exaggerations of surprise, shock, disbelief, irritation—whatever seemed demanded by the piercing looks thrown them by others in the audience. How could *Kiley Himself* not know?

"Now hold it!" the man shouted. "I asked a question. I've got the floor."

The gabble subsided to a surly rumble.

"That's better. Mister Kiley? I'm not being critical. Merely curious." The man's voice wore a new edge, smoother, sharper, vaguely antagonistic.

The buzz took on a different tone as people rose from their seats to get a better view of the speaker.

"You'll have to understand," Kiley said. "I've been away so long, and. . . ." He looked to Jackie for help. She was motioning for him to sit down.

"I only asked because I'm wondering whether you understand the negative impulse behind talking black. It seems to many of us—"

A chorus of boos drowned the man's words, and shouts of "Bizad!" "Get him out!" "Where'd he come from?" filled the hall.

Before Kiley could react, Jackie grabbed his hand and dragged him stumbling from the stage.

"What's going—"

"Not now, man!" she snapped. "It's gon be a lynchin if we ain't get shed of this place. Somebody done plant that mothah just to stir a ruccus. If we ain't shag ass right now, you gon get caught in the middle."

He hobbled along beside her as fast as his blocks could carry him.

11

"Some of our colleagues would cling to the discriminatory practice of 'grading' students' performances. A good teacher does not need the threat of grades to earn response from his class; a teacher who grades his students is a poor teacher."

The Kiley Proposal

NINE UU SENIORS stood at attention before the antiquated Mack towtruck and wheezed in unison. Nine pairs of nose plugs swelled nostrils above nine pairs of sealed lips. A hint of green flickered behind the clotted gray clouds overhead and marked the university forcefield dome. None of the boys or girls looked up.

They stared rapt at Dr. Hobart Reid, who glared back at them through the goggles of his gas mask. The time had come. Field test.

Of the nine children drawn up in rigid file, only three could be chosen for graduate school. Six would be rejected. All nine would receive an "A" on today's test, of course, but six would fail. And they knew that.

Reid was a tough one. He might even deny the B.S. to some of the failing six, although he didn't make a practice of such severity. The three who passed today would carry through life the imprimatur of Hobart Reid. His okay could make a career. He was the senior man in the UU Transportation Department; his was the voice that mattered.

Reid had joined the university faculty straight from Ferrous U., where his pioneering work in Engine Repair had drawn accolades from progressive educators throughout Detroit. It was he who had instituted the program of providing free engine tune-ups to residents of the community surrounding Ferrous U., in order to give his students practical experience in gasket-changing.

From that success, a proven innovator, Hobart Reid had come to Urban U., trailing clouds of glory, enticed by the offer of the Edsel Chair in Higher Transportation. He boarded the sealed, windowless train within the Ferrous U. forcefield shell, spent the nine-hour journey listening to his own books, and debouched within the confines of Urban U. It was as if he had not left home.

Not one to rest upon his reputation, he had since authored two respected driver education tapes and was consultant to service-station managers throughout the university. That was the man the nine students must impress.

He tugged on his pigskin driving gloves and smiled at them.

They didn't know that. His mask covered his mouth and nose. "Weeillrgh?" he asked.

"Okay, Hobie," the students chanted.

"Hrrstffl!" He pointed at the first in line.

Jimmie Brown towered over the other seniors. He was five-foot-two and was suspected of having grown during his six undergraduate years, though no one could prove it. His admissions records were written rather than taped—an archaic practice no longer allowed—and therefore inaccessible to most Fac administrators. But, growing or not, he was five-foot-two, and his imposing appearance depressed the other students.

Reid handed Jimmie the ignition key.

Jimmie jumped onto the running board and slid inside the cab. His feet reached the clutch and brake pedals, and he sighed with relief. Nervously, he inserted and turned the ignition key. The engine groaned, clanked, clattered, turned over, and caught. He depressed the clutch and engaged the gears.

The truck leaped like a startled refrigerator. It stalled.

Reid frowned. Several of the waiting students smiled, without letting their lips part. But too soon. Jimmie started the truck again, and this time succeeded. He drove slowly down the limestone test track, cautiously negotiated two right turns, and backed into position before the simulated abandoned car. He lowered the tow boom and waited.

Reid nodded approval.

Jimmie raced the engine with joy. He guided the truck back to the starting point, again making two perfect right turns. For a moment he debated shifting to second. It was then that inspiration seized him.

The bold will appreciate his courage.

He drove past the starting point!

Aghast, the other eight students stared slack-jawed. To come so near success, and then to fail!

How little they understood. Jimmie had passed the mark intentionally. He shifted into reverse, cramped the large steering wheel—and parallel parked!

Shocked at Jimmie's arrogance, half-fearful of Dr. Reid's reaction, the students drew themselves to attention and concentrated on shallow breathing.

Reid shook his head in admiration. Gutsy kid, he thought. Not even a grad student, and parallel parking on his own.

He gave a thumbs-up.

The waiting students sagged. They could never surpass that. Now only two fellowships remained for the contending eight. They glared mutual hatred at Jimmie as he swaggered back to join them in line. One of the girls, Tricia Neely, began to cry.

"Grrmmsmpfl?" Reid shouted through his mask.

The exam went on.

12

INSTEAD OF RETURNING to the hospital through the tunnels that honeycombed the building foundations, Jackie gave Kiley a gas mask and led him to the surface. "Ain't nobody see us goin back this way."

He tugged at his mask straps and squinted toward the bilious sun high overhead. He had found that by shuffling along rather than lifting his blocks he could keep pace with Jackie's rapid stride. Like an ice skater, he swooped and glided over the pavement.

They crossed Urban Boulevard, with the university subway vibrating beneath them. To his left he noticed a large field covered with artificial turf where he saw several young children watching a truck drive in tight little squares. A block later he looked back but could no longer see them. He felt like Bulldog Drummond, walking into the fog.

Buildings rose on all sides, high-rise housing as well as classrooms, but he could not point to a demarcation line between university and neighborhood. The two had merged in his absence to create a hybrid. A mixture of the old and the new, the area through which they passed was not the city of the future he expected to see. It remained a slum, different from his recollections only in that now it seemed deserted. His memory peopled these streets with jostling bodies. Now he saw no one, none of the shoppers, no idle strollers. Here and there a university guard stood in a doorway and waved his cattle prod by way of greeting. That was all.

Another distinction impressed itself on him. No graffiti. These walls should have been covered with gang names, slogans, or boredom recorded as four-letter challenges to the serenity of passers-by. No graffiti. In its stead were crude sketches, many sexual in implication but less blatant than the simple thrust of vocabulary.

A massive, windowless concrete block of a building before them caught his eye. "What's that one?" he shouted through his mask.

"Lounge." Jackie pointed to a picture on the corner of the building. It showed a chair, worked in triangular mosaic tiles but unmistakably a chair. "For screwin off between classes," she said. "Students only. We go this way."

She continued down a narrow alley.

Each building they passed bore a mosaic pictograph at eye level. Some were easy to interpret. For others, he would need a Rosetta Stone. He recognized a painter's easel, a set of stylized bowling pins, a shoe (?), and a diapered baby. The baby was flecked green and gold, with a sparkling blue smile wavering randomly across its face. On one building he saw what looked to him like a phallus. It's hard to say whether he saw it as such because it was a phallus, or because a week of abstinent proximity to Jackie's warmth had colored his perceptions.

"Liberry!" she shouted over her shoulder.

The pictograph on this building was more complex than the others. It showed a reel of recording tape spilling into a mound from which rose a scroll. On the scroll was a real word. LIBRARY. Kiley started to ask. . . .

"Compromise," she said. "It's what Morgan wanted, 'cause Bizads come up with half the money, 'sall."

He nodded as though he understood.

He followed her through a curtain of rushing air into the hospital foyer. Vacuum and sonics sucked and throbbed around them, and Kiley felt his fillings turn to ice, then lava, then they were through, their gas masks hung on hooks at the doorway behind them, their clothes cleansed of airborne contamination.

Unconsciously, out of habit, he ran his fingers through his remembered hair and over a slick scalp. "Now can you explain the commotion back there, at the press conference?"

"It's three or four peoples got in where they ain't belong, 'sall. Leave it to them Bizads. They tryin to sneak a march on the rest of us."

"You make less sense—"

"I'm sayin it, ain't I? They wants me to be fair, let you see all sides 'fore you chooses which way you gon jump. And that's where I been at. Only fair's fair. Soon's you learn what's goin down, I knows you gon pick Fac. I'm just waitin till you can get it together."

"Why *me?* What have I got to do with—"

"We gon do this right," Jackie interrupted. "Things comin thick and fast now, and we ain't baby you no more." She seized his arm and urged him toward a room whose door was decorated with another of the stylized designs he had seen outside.

This one shimmered in three dimensions as he approached it— a starkly black-and-white spiral that seemed to suck him down toward a center he could not quite see. Something lay at the pit of the visual whirlpool, inviting, tantalizing, not a scene itself but the implication of a scene.

Inside the room, Jackie led him to a chair that faced a similar spiral on the far wall.

He sat, and watched the spiral whirl a spectrum of shifting colors. The colors drew him down, and in, and away. . . .

13

KILEY ABSORBED a history.

He did not see pictures. Neither did he hear voices. He experienced a whirl of sensations that translated themselves into a gestalt. He was in, and was with, and was of a scope/span/segment of experience that something deep in his being told him was "past." He shared it as a contemporary, yet sensed its pastness. Certain nexes of sensation-fact-event struck roots in Kiley's memory; others were lost on his inability to relate them to experiences he had known in his own, interrupted, life. Make machines efficient as you will, any history remains idiosyncratic.

An hour after Jackie pushed him into the chair and activated the spiral of colors, Kiley knew:

Right-wing political reaction to student excesses of the sixties and seventies makes of the university an "enemy of the people," as defined by "the people" (i.e., everyone outside the university). Voters refuse to fund what they consider hotbeds of un-American radicalism and they blind themselves to the pogrom they secretly approve and tacitly allow. Hardhats attack the universities.

And so do ghetto blacks.

And so do ghetto whites.

And so do right-thinking academics themselves.

As if universities really were THE ENEMY. As if they exist independent of the attackers.

Blacks burn the buildings that day by day encroach on the teeming neighborhoods they hate and are permitted to populate.

Hardhats, who built those buildings and are building more in the brief intervals between strikes, beat those doing the burning.

Politicians call out various law-enforcement agencies, ranging upward in power from local police to National Guard, ranging downward in efficiency from local police to National Guard.

Law-enforcement agencies follow time-hallowed tradition and stop the bloodshed by shooting the burners, and the beaters, and many of the silent observers, and not a few of the FBI agents who have infiltrated all involved groups and participate in the burning, and the beating, and the shooting.

It is a confusing time. Till rational heads prevail.

A compromise is struck. Academics already involved in fostering

internal reform promise to clean their own fouled nests, given sufficient time and money. A stalemate, you might say.

But a timely ill wind blows across Asia and sweeps before it
racism at least as virulent as that which, all agree, infects America:
China attacks the Soviet Union. For two weeks, five thousand miles
of horizon glows a brilliant orange, as though Howard Johnson were
roofing a continent. When the fallout settles over a glazed desert,
many problems have been solved. The cliché about ill winds proves
true.

There is no hunger in Asia.

There is no longer a threat from the International Communist
Conspiracy.

There are 20 percent fewer people in the world.

There is no longer a reason to blame only the automobile and
American manufacturing for the particulate filth that hovers in the
atmosphere (and, incidentally, raises the global mean temperature a
full degree during the first postwar year; the polar ice caps begin
to melt).

There is no longer the need to invest some 70 percent of the
American GNP in defense.

The federal government, with excess tax revenue in hand, an-
nounces an all-out war on inadequate education. Educators who have
filed tentative requests for a few thousand dollars find those requests
honored with millions—on the condition that the university continue in the path marked out by those within academe who promise
to solve all social problems.

Each urban concentration of a size sufficient to contain a vola-
tile, uncontrollable ghetto population becomes a university. It does
not "contain." It *becomes*. Sixty-one American cities with a population of more than a quarter million *become* universities, renamed,
enclosed, subsidized, and isolated.

And of these the first is Urban University. Here, full democracy
in education is born. Here are demonstrated the merits of open
enrollment, the abolition of grading systems and of faculty repression of students. Here gather all those committed to the goals of the

new university—full support, full educational choice, full employment, full care of the surrounding community, which lacks the experience and wisdom found only within the university.

And of Urban University may be said, its prophet nonpareil is the martyred Robert Kiley, author of *The Kiley Proposal*.

On a cenotaph rising high above Kiley Avenue in the smog-shrouded air near the center of the eighty-eight-square-mile Urban U. campus is a plaque. It reads: HE BUILDED BETTER THAN HE KNEW.

Ten years after the dedication of that cenotaph, the plaque is removed and transferred to the basement of Kiley House, which contains his former office. In its stead, since that day, a loop tape has announced—every thirty seconds (half around the dial by the fastest hand), "He builded better than he knew."

People are born into the university, are fed, housed, clothed, trained or educated, medicated, bedded, wedded, delivered, employed, promoted or demoted, churched, cherished, retired, euthanized, embalmed, cremated, buried or recycled—all within the confines of the university.

They never leave.

For that is the compromise. No interference with the university by the public "outside"; no interference with the real world by members of the university. Never in the history of mankind have so many people been educated to such useful and productive lives.

And of all this is Robert Kiley the architect, in achieved fact and in the collective mind of the university, if not in intention. He is The Father of the University.

An hour after Jackie had pushed him into the chair and activated the spiral of colors, he understood his new eminence.

It made him want to blush with pride. You can't blush intentionally.

"You startin to get some of it now?" Jackie asked.

"I think so," he said. "But I'm not *really* as important as that record implies." He favored her with a smile and lowered his eyes modestly. "I'm just a simple—"

"Sheet, man! I know what you are. None of that matter. It's what people *think* you are." Jackie will always be honest with him. "Right now, Facreps and Bizads is likely workin out ways to get you choosin sides. Appropriations time comin on, and with you in their corner, each one of them figure to get their hand deeper in the pot.

"All you got to do is keep your mouth shut and listen. I spoze be makin you all hot to go Fac, where you belongs. Bengston and them figurin ways to stop that. Maybe you ain't much by your own self, only you the bone all them dogs fightin over. If Bizads has their way, they gon fuck up everything we got shakin here. They waitin to rap on it with you. So come along, only keep from agreein till you hears both sides. Dig?"

Kiley smiled at her agitation. Obviously she was jealous of his importance in the new scheme of things. The official history he now knew defined his importance.

Morgan knows a different history of Urban U., one that Kiley would not enjoy experiencing.

14

"[A good] argument for passing [the] proposal: under the present [repressive] system, our best students [are] not interested in teaching careers. Improve the system, attract the best."

> *The Notebooks of Robert Kiley*
> (as edited)

CARLETON FLOY sat trembling at his desk. His office looked out on Kiley Avenue and stood directly across from Kiley House. The proximity of that name, the position of his office, had always made Floy feel a scrutiny that didn't exist in fact. These past few days he had suffered even greater pressure. Kiley himself was alive again; he who was dead had risen. To Carleton Floy it could mean only one thing. He was about to be examined.

Only weeks earlier he might have faced such a possibility calmly. He had climbed out of the ghetto, joined the power structure, was assimilated. He spun in his chair to glance for reassurance at the diploma framed and hung on the wall. All those squigglies said "Master of Science"—he had memorized the shapes and could print the words himself. He reached up and pressed the button mounted in the corner of the gilt frame, then leaned back to relax as the soothing voice recited. "The trustees of Urban University, upon nomination of the faculty, have confered upon Carleton Floy the degree of Master of Science, in recognition of. . . ."

The floorboards creaked behind him, and he jerked around in panic. It was only one of his students. He handed her a paper cup of water and her daily Retardo, placed a pencil mark next to her picture on his roll sheet, and watched to make certain that she swallowed. As she left, he checked his watch—on his black wrist a glistening chromium lozenge, a graduation present from his block dean some twenty-two years before. The little slow hand was on the big 3; the bigger hand was on the little 15. Instantly he knew it was 3:15. Only one more hour and one more fifteen before he could close his office and go home. But twelve of his students had not yet picked up their Retardos. Among the twelve, his son, Tyrone.

That was Carleton Floy's guilty secret. His son was a deviant. Unknown to Carleton's superiors, Tyrone had begun to pubesce.

Carleton stared at his son's picture on the roll sheet and tried to persuade himself that the flesh-and-blood Tyrone still looked the same: downy cheeks, bright eyes, youthful innocence. The pretense failed. He could not blank out the memory of what he had seen at the breakfast table. Tyrone, reaching for the yeast spread; his arm stretched forth; the faint hint of hair in the boy's armpit. And Tyrone only nineteen.

All day he had tried to delude himself. "Shadow," he muttered again.

He knew better. Tyrone was pubescing. If the block dean discovered it, there went Tyrone's future, obliterated by the rage of his rampant hormones. No more education, consignment to the Buildings and Grounds Department, never to rise above Instructor of Maintenance—that was Tyrone's bleak future, should the truth get out.

Carleton Floy lied with his pencil and placed a check mark beside Tyrone's picture. Twenty-two years on the faculty, and now reduced to this. Cheating! Assistant Professor of Hygiene, entrusted with the daily Retardos for twenty-five students, an honorable man committed to the ideals of higher education, Carleton Floy glanced sadly through his window at Kiley House.

He laid his head on his arms and wept bitter tears.

15

"[Several] nits in the Business School [are] bound to fight the proposal. [They] don't seem interested in students[' personality development and self-realization] anyway."

> *The Notebooks of Robert Kiley*
> (as edited)

REAL WOOD PANELING covered three walls of the Business Administration principal conference room. The fourth wall was punctured by an apparatus that seemed half cathode tube, half pigsnout. It was the holographic projector, through which links to any classroom in the Business School might be effected. (No one inside Urban U. understood it, of course, but several of them knew which buttons to push to make it operate. A crew from Washington had installed it, left careful instructions on its use, and scampered out of the university with great relief.)

A button was pushed, and the apparatus began to function.

The apparitions of Robert Kiley, M.A., and Jacqueline Muller, Ph.D. (*honoris causa*) flitted through the snout nostrils and appeared to solidify at one side of a long conference table. Also of wood. Bizads have lush budgets.

Across the table from these holographic projections sat Dr. Howard Bengston and his staff.

In a white-tiled room within the UU Labs Complex, Hospital Building, Kiley and Jackie sat in form-fitting sponge chairs and stared at Bengston, his staff, and his conference table, all of which had just materialized before them in three-dimensional living color, stereophonic sound, and modulated arrogance.

"Welcome, Mister Kiley," Bengston said. He was jovial, expansive, determined to control the day's proceedings.

"Welcome your own self," Jackie muttered. She concentrated on appearing neutral while functioning as Fac observer to a meeting whose outcome she feared. Bengston had Morgan's ear, had cajoled several real doctors and scientists into entering the university to resurrect Kiley, and seemed practiced at intellectual seduction. She was afraid of his persuading Kiley to join the Bizads in their machinations.

"I won't josh with you, Mister Kiley. I feel it's best if we lie our cards on the table, like they say." Bengston glanced at his colleagues and waited for their nods of agreement. He got them. He was the chairman.

"Right, then. Well. Now that you've had the chance to look around, how do you like what you've seen?"

Kiley shrugged. "What can I say, Doctor Bengston? I haven't seen much except the inside of this place."

Bengston aimed a frown at Jackie, then tried a new tack. "Call me Howie, why don't you?"

His staff stifled a gasp. It *was* rather shocking. Traditionally, the privilege of using first names was restricted to students. Not a Bizad in the entire university would dare such familiarity with Howard Bengston. Clearly, the old man was pulling out all stops.

"He connin you," Jackie leaned close to whisper.

"Okay, Howie. Can we get on with things here? I understand you're about to persuade me to join the Business School faculty. Is that it?"

Bengston flustered. "Who said anything . . . ? I can't. . . .

Look, Bob. Let me spell it out. It's not a matter of joining one faculty or another, you know? It's more like deciding where your best interests lay, with whom your future is most secure . . . with. And I only want the chance to show you the educational directions that seem most promising to we Bizads. To use the vernacular. You know?"

"All I know is that I'm supposed to help with funding. That's what—"

"Doctor Muller told you, I suppose." Bengston shook a playful finger at Jackie and tried to retract his bulging eyes. "Naughty, naughty there, Doctor. You've been misleading our patient again, haven't you?"

The man to Bengston's right, his secretary, Dr. Noble, slid a piece of paper along the table into Bengston's sight. "Bleeding heart broad," it read.

Bengston nodded and donned his smile again, this time with visible effort. "All we're asking for is a fair chance to define a few theoretical differences between the outmoded Fac program and the visionary—but practical, notice that—visionary but practical ideas that characterize your best thinking, educationwise, today.

"Now. Here's an example. You can read, can't you, Bob?"

Kiley nodded.

"And you've found it to your advantage, I feel. All we're saying here is that we would like more of our students trained in that same skill. Call it *avant-garde*. That doesn't matter much. But whenever we get students who want to go into management, we've got to start with them like they've never been through anything you might call school in their life. That's not efficient, dammit! Just not efficient. Maybe I shouldn't try and pin you down like this, but I'm giving you the kernel, Bobby. The very heart and soul of the matter. Most of us here"—his sweeping arms took in the group sitting at the table with him—"grew up with our alphabet and came to love it, you know?"

Noble nudged Bengston again and whispered something.

"Right." Bengston pointed toward a boy at the end of the table.

"But some of us came to an understanding as adults. Doctor Feenan, there, for example."

Dr. Feenan rose and took a bow. Because he was only five-foot-one—a Retardo addict and still prepubescent—he bowed out of sight beneath the table edge.

"Let Doctor Feenan explain what it means, not having the skills needful to a rich career in management."

"Who's Feenan?" Kiley leaned toward Jackie to ask.

"Search me."

He couldn't help smiling. That was still one of his ambitions. And what woman could refuse The Father of the University? He began to envision all sorts of benefits to be derived from his new desirability. Fac wanted him, Bizads wanted him. Now if Jackie. . . .

". . . listening, Mister Kiley?"

"Watch it, Feenan," Bengston snapped.

"No. He's right. I'm sorry, Doctor Feenan. What were you saying?"

In a voice that shifted from tenor to bass at unexpected moments, Feenan repeated himself. "Merely making the point that it's not so much fun coming up through the ranks, then finding out you've been taught a bunch of worthless shieEE—" A squeak interrupted him in midsyllable. He continued with a new baritone under tentative control. "I intend only to be factual, Mister Kiley. When I got sense enough to transfer schools, a previous administration was in charge here. I was taught to read under methadone reward-withdrawal, you understand? That was before Doctor Bengston helped us shift entirely to the Neo-Behaviorist approach to learning basic skills."

"Fine, Doctor Feenan. Well said, my boy." Bengston preened.

Noble pushed another scrap of paper under Bengston's eyes, then slid his chair back from the table and left the room.

"Good-oh," Bengston said. "I see we're ready, Bob. I wanted to let you in on two of our current learning methods. We don't rely on drugs any longer. It always was a touchy sort of program, what with complications. You take your average kid on Retardo, then dose him with methadone, it does something to the glands."

Heads at the conference table swung to stare at the flame-red Dr. Feenan.

"Just so," Bengston nodded. "Really screws up a guy's love life, if you catch my meaning. Lots of parties, but no balls. You know?"

Nearly everyone at the table laughed at Bengston's sally.

"Crude mothah," Jackie whispered.

"So we've reached back to the classical masters of learning theory and adapted methods known when you were alive. Uh—that's not to say you're not alive *now*, but. . . ." Bengston blinked in bewilderment and trailed off into momentary silence. "Well. Suppose we just transfer you over and let you see for yourself."

Bengston's hand reached toward a bank of switches on the tabletop, and

16

KILEY GASPED as the floor dropped out from under him. He seized the chair arms and squeezed his eyes shut against the vertigo that clawed at his stomach and threatened to reject his last meal.

Slowly he cracked one eyelid. Through the fringe of lash he saw Jackie seated comfortably beside him, neither disturbed nor surprised. Her serenity gave him strength. He opened the other eye and looked for "Up" and "Down."

Bengston and his staff had disappeared. In their stead, before Kiley now in an area he wanted to believe was the same hospital room, yawned a large auditorium. His eyes focused at length on a stage far below, and then his chair joined the holograph camera in a slow zoom in on the scene below. Echoing in the background, as though sounded from inside a barrel, came Bengston's voice.

"Notice the students there, Bob. We're teaching them to copy out a paragraph."

Three boys sat beside a long table, under the gaze of a pacing instructor. Each held a stylus in his right hand. From the top of the stylus a small wire curved around the wrist and swooped to the tabletop. Before each of the boys stood a book, propped open and erect.

"Real books, Bob. And you might be interested to know, they're copies of *The Kiley Proposal*. How about that?"

Before Kiley could speak, Jackie said, "Mind if I asks them is it always that book they copies?"

"You're *observing*, Doctor Muller. I would appreciate it if you wouldn't interrupt." Bengston spoke with offended dignity dripping from each icy, measured syllable. "To be perfectly honest, Bob, they do work with other texts. But I'm sure you understand that, right? Right, Bob?"

"Sure. I understand. But why copy something? Why not simply have them write?"

"Ahhh! I was hoping you'd ask that. Doctor Noble? Are you there yet?"

Onto the stage walked Noble, breathless from apparently having run some distance. "Yes sir. I'll get it."

He walked over, pushed the instructor aside, and reached across one of the student's shoulders to lift the sheet of paper on which the boy had been writing. Beneath the paper lay a thin leaf of copper on which lines had been etched. "This is the master," he explained. "The paragraph the students are copying has already been imposed on this template. Now, their task is to write on the paper and duplicate the paths indicated here." His moving forefinger traced a line of cursive script across the copper template. "Let me show you the result.

"You." Noble tapped the second student on the shoulder. "Keep writing, and do it good."

As the student wrote, Noble cupped one ear in pantomime.

Kiley strained forward in his chair, and heard it. Melody, faint chimes, the silver thrill of a celeste twinkled in the air. "Okay," he said. "I got it."

"Make a mistake," Noble ordered the student. "Don't worry. It's on the first program."

The boy's hand swerved from the proper path, and a foghorn blatted in protest.

Kiley knew he ought to be impressed, but the whole charade was beginning to bore him. "All right," he said. "They do it one way, they hear something pretty. Another way—"

"Hold on there, Bob," Bengston's disembodied voice interrupted. "I don't think you get the full implications. Not only does the student have to copy the words accurately. He has to copy the *script*, too, if he wants to stay on the lines. We teach penmanship!"

Jackie wore a worried look that faded when she recognized Kiley's lack of interest. "Thank you, Doctor Bengston. Now we maybe—"

"And here's the real clincher," Noble shouted, waving at the camera. He flipped a switch on the tabletop. "Program two, boy. Do it good."

The student once more hunched over his stylus and began laboriously to draw the required letters. Celeste music tinkled pleasantly in the air.

"Now. Make a mistake," Noble ordered.

The boy shook his head and continued to write.

"Make a mistake, I said!"

When the student ignored him, Noble gingerly reached out one hand to jostle the boy's elbow.

"HUUUHHHHH!!!" The boy's head snapped back and his body arched in spasm.

"See it?" Noble roared triumphantly. "We hit him with a hundred and thirty volts, every time he goes off the line." He nodded to the instructor, who switched off the current; and the boy sagged low in his chair.

"I tell you, Bobby. You learn real fast that way, and no mistake," Bengston said. "We can take a kid who doesn't know A from B, and inside of two weeks, they're copying things better than you or I could."

"Good Christ! That kid looked like he broke his back!"

"Sure, it hurt." A sulking note fluttered in Bengston's answer. "But you don't make a chicken without breaking eggs."

"Let's get the chicken's opinion," Kiley muttered. He felt a warm touch on his wrist. Jackie had reached over to pat his hand and was smiling at him.

"WAIT!" Bengston shouted. "We're not done! Noble! You get over to the 'Stimucenter.' Understand?"

Kiley didn't hear the answer. He was too busy closing his eyes against the confusion that sprang up as again the room swirled and tilted before him. The auditorium faded to gray at his feet. His motionless chair stuttered through stroboscopic black-white patches and came to rest in

17

a lounge.

A circle of twenty strangely shaped chairs surrounded a small console where a fat man stared at something out of Kiley's range of vision. Each chair was topped by a pair of forward-reaching wings that hid a student's head in shadow. The room was a riot of colors, electric blue, shading to magenta and scarlet, random blots of yellow splashed on the curving walls. It looked designed to drive people's eyes within the shaded protection of the chairwings, if only to escape nausea. In every chair a body lay reclining, visible from the waist down—twenty pairs of trousered legs, forty black socks, forty shined cordovan oxfords.

"They're all boys," Kiley said, surprised. "Like the other place."

"*Now* you startin to get it on." Jackie clapped her hands in delight. "Sexist bastards, every one of them Bizads. When you see girl one in their classes, you let me know." She nodded her head vehemently. "Why else does you think Bengston, he so shook I'm the one get to look after you?"

"Maybe I do see—"

"Here we are again, Bob. This is the most interesting of the both of the experiments, I feel. See all these students? They're reading! Out loud. There's a mike pickup in the chair heads, and as long as they read right, and keep the right pace, they match a program playing in the master console there. And these boys *want* to learn. Nobody's forcing them, no punishment. I'm not apologizing, by the way. Pain has its uses. But like I often remind myself, 'Doctor Bengston. The anticipation of reward is a far more evocative stimulus than the mere avoidance of pain.'" He droned like a child in catechism.

"What reward?"

Bengston chuckled. "I can see you like to get right to the core of the matter. You'll have to trust me on this one, Bobby. I can't *show* you what they're enjoying, but I can promise you they are.

"Noble? Doctor Noble! Where the hell is that. . . . ? There you are. What are you stalling around for?"

Noble staggered to a splay-legged halt in the center of the room. "Iwa . . . eewa . . . Iwa. . . ." He stood panting like an emphysemic glassblower. After a moment, he gasped, "Uhwa . . . uhwa . . . uh-what comes . . . un, next?"

"Get one of those kids on his feet. I want Mister Kiley to see the electrodes."

Noble hoisted one of the flaccid bodies and held him erect. The boy continued to focus glazed eyes on the calfbound copy of *Reader's Digest* he held open before him. He mumbled inaudibly. Slowly, his eyes slid off the page toward Noble. Then, without speaking, he struggled to return to the chair.

Noble held him and peered at the boy's scalp. He shouted over his shoulder, "Let me have number thirty-five!"

The fat man ran his hands over the console, and the student ceased his struggles.

"Right here." Noble pointed to a small silver knob on the boy's scalp. "The other end of this electrode is planted in the anterior pleasure center of the brain. A slight stimulation with broadcast current, and he thinks he's in heaven."

"That's the secret, Bob-oh," Bengston said. "I don't know exactly what he feels, but he sure as hell likes it. The better he reads, the more juice we give him. If he starts falling off, off goes the current. Simple as that—no pain, just deprivation of pleasure."

Kiley searched through his muddled thoughts. Somewhere he had the nagging feeling that he ought to disapprove of the method. But he didn't know why. "If it works teaching him to read—"

"Exactly!" Bengston shouted. "It'll work for *anything!* And not only on the kids. We can take an adult and give him perpetual orgasm. What do you think of that?"

"Isn't that a little—"

"But these kids, they're too young."

Kiley turned to Jackie. "I thought he was working with university students."

"He is. Only they on Retardo."

"Have you seen enough, Bob?" Bengston asked.

"Now, wait a minute. I've seen what you're doing. But don't you need to explain *why?* You make it sound as though those kids won't get any education short of the conditioning you're giving them."

"That's the case. You've got it perfectly. Glad you see it our way, Bob-oh. I'll get cracking on the budget. Be talking to you."

The hospital room snapped back into existence. This time the shock scarcely bothered Kiley. One minute he was surrounded by glaring colors—the next, white walls swooped in to enclose him. He loosened his death grip on the chair arms and waited for Jackie to speak.

She was waiting, too, standing now, ready to refute whatever he might say.

"I guess I'm going to get the Fac sales pitch next. Is that it?"

She smiled warmly enough to start his chilled blood moving freely. "They *didn't* convince you, did they?"

She bent over him and cupped his chin in her hand, raised his face to hers, and kissed him.

For a moment he felt out of character. *He* should have been the one to make the move, not Jackie. He had nowhere to put his hands. Her searching blue eyes seemed to read his thoughts, so he stopped thinking.

It's called nonelectroencephalographic stimulation. Bizads will not yet have discovered the secret.

18

DR. JACQUELINE MULLER will be a difficult person to categorize, for those who take comfort in categories. She can best be inadequately described as a "committer." Mere "joiners" become Elks, Red Cross canvassers, Peace Corps dropouts, and hypochondriacs. "Committers" are different; they become the archetypal Elk, organizers of Red Cross canvassing drives, Peace Corps re-enlistees, and volunteers for medical experimentation. A "committer" who converts to Roman Catholicism eschews meat after Thursday noon, in spite of new practices in the Church. One who quits smoking hides the ashtrays and spends his idle hours seeking out smoke-filled rooms in which to cough with patient martyrdom. Jackie Muller is a "committer."

Her parents deserve the credit. They had never shown any belief stronger than a vague preference for some sunshiny days over certain rainy days. Of course she had rebelled against their placid peace by committing herself to causes and crusades. Often two or three in the same day.

Her parents deserve credit in other ways. They had raised her themselves, in nearly total isolation, high atop a fire lookout tower in the Montana forest wilderness. For several miles in any direction, there was nothing but trees. Her father daily patrolled the fence surrounding the preserve he guarded. Her mother made a weekly trek to the gate to fetch in supplies delivered from the nearest supermarket. And when done with those slight duties, they taught little Jackie to fantasize.

She had named every tree in the forest. She looked for birds with broken wings in order to heal them. (Often her father broke a bird's wing and left it where she might find it.) She read all the Albert Payson Terhune dog books, and believed them. She developed a selective understanding of her forest paradise. When she stumbled across the maggot-infested body of a dead squirrel, she saw only the feasting, shining white maggots, and thrilled at their happiness. When she accompanied her father on his daily patrol of the forest perimeter, she didn't notice him stripping used condoms from the cyclone fencing or hear him hurling curses at the picnickers outside; her eyes focused only on the beauties inside her natural playground.

It was therefore inevitable that she should come to harm, once loosed upon the world. She forgave her first three seducers but eventually grew chary of her favor. Brighter, better-educated, endowed with more human feeling than any man she met in the rural library where she worked, she set out for a city.

No city would admit her. She had been born too late. Each city was by then a university, already populated by persons born there and by those who had entered by choice before the forcefield shells went up to create the taxpayer-approved isolation.

Those had been hectic days, all unknown to Jackie in her forest fastness. Like the landrush on the Oklahoma territories nearly a century before, the rush into, and out of, the newly designated universities was a stampede. Into the universities poured those committed to the plight of the cities, social workers, persons seeking unlimited welfare support, and persons eager to administer such huge sums—anyone, in fact, who chose to enter. For whatever reason. Out of the universities poured professionals of all sorts, slumlords, skilled technicians, emphysemics—anyone, in fact, who could see beyond tomorrow. Then the forcefields were activated.

One master switch in Washington closed, and America became a paradise. Small-town taxpayers saw the clouds again, reveled in the clean air, the placid, calm countryside, the absence of agitators who had formerly disturbed their serenity. Such luxury seemed cheap at the price (a 40 percent, across-the-board, income tax). The new order offered other benefits as well. Soon no one entered the universities any longer, except for public charges sent there—the indigent, criminals, all the unwashed.

But Jackie didn't know that. And the few persons who might have helped her enter a university took pity on her ignorance. They lied and told her there was no way.

Jackie found a town. The distinction between a town and a city is merely a matter of government subsidy. In that town was a college —old-fashioned, quiet, a nineteenth-century haven from adulthood. She attended the college and with some self-conscious embarrassment studied French and biology (she had read about a real university and knew how irrelevent were such studies, but she had to make do with the world she found). In that same town she joined three different churches consecutively, then withdrew from all three when she found herself simultaneously committed to two opposing faiths.

She drifted into an archaic chapter of Women's Lib. "Archaic" because, in every university, Women's Lib had long since achieved, or abandoned, all its goals. In Jackie's small town it still wore the air of revolution, and she drew strength from the principles expressed at weekly testifying sessions. She left the chapter—still committed to the principles learned there—after a disagreement with Ms. Cleotis Bench, chapter presidentess. Technically, she was expelled after Cleotis had observed her neglecting to coldcock a man who thoughtlessly opened a door for her. More to the point, she and Cleotis had suffered a personal disagreement over what method of achieving orgasm was most acceptable. Actually, she had coldcocked Cleotis in the shower room of the YM&WCA.

She went to work in an orphanage, and it was there that she discovered her entree to the university. Orphans not adopted after six weeks at the local orphanage were sent to the nearest university to be raised in the Department of Child Care. She falsified the proper forms, had herself declared an orphan, and committed herself to Urban University.

She wanted to help.

They discovered that she could read. She was given an honorary Doctorate of Child Care and made an Assistant Professor. Her commitment to Faculty ideals and her losing campaign in a Facrep election gained her widespread attention. When she heard the rumors about Robert Kiley, love for an ideal fired her imagination. She became the university's leading expert on Kiley's past, and the logical choice to guide and care for his future.

After all, wouldn't it be like raising a child?

She thought so.

In the short time she has known him, her love for what he represents has scarcely diminished, although she grows less and less fond of what he is.

Or *had* grown, until the aforementioned unpremeditated kiss. With that act, she once more committed herself. Her reading had taught her that many a weak man has been saved from himself by the love of a good woman. Books like that will still be available. Her breast swelled with pride at the thought of what he, through her help, might yet become.

None of this factual background should be considered in any way derogatory or final. For Jackie Muller, too, is still becoming. The number of ideas or causes to which she has not yet committed herself beggars the imagination.

We find her, then, on a plateau—a long road behind her, several paths ahead, to choose among as she will. Graven on the basalt foundations of that plateau are the words that spell out her mission: the care and nurture of Robert Kiley.

And the hell with Cleotis Bench.

19

"How did a guy like me get involved in this? Hearings [are] half done, and [one is] still not sure what they mean [a characteristically modest passage]."

The Notebooks of Robert Kiley
(as edited)

THE FAC LOUNGE buzzed with activity. A number of elected Facreps were there, along with members of the Faculty-at-Large. Students in the Department of Catering were clearing away trays of half-emptied dishes. A field representative of the Department of Personal Sundries circulated among the Fac, selling after-dinner mints and cigarettes (unfiltered, high-tar and -nicotine cigarettes only—as required by HEW Combined U-Fed Experimental Project 615a). The salesgirl took from each customer his ID card, slipped it into her beltrecorder, and charged the purchase price against his monthly stipend. In one corner of the crowded room a kalimba quartet entertained themselves and perhaps three of the fifty-odd people who endured every note they twanged.

Kiley entered to a burst of applause. He and Jackie had eaten in his room in order to avoid mobs like this one, and to savor the silent warmth they had begun to share. Refreshed, restored, able to walk without his cane, Kiley felt ready to face his colleagues. They were his own people, unlike the Bizads who had tried to enlist his eminence merely for their own selfish ends. He looked forward to the rest of the evening, now that he had begun to understand his new circumstances.

"Almost like a homecoming," he said loudly. He thought: *courting time.*

Fac seated nearest the front of the room nodded. Two spokesmen rose from a couch and came to greet him, hands outstretched: Dr. Barnes, the angry black he had met in the hospital, and another man he didn't recognize. Like Barnes, the stranger wore a dashiki, and his sunburst of orange hair matched Barnes' jet corona in bulk and splendor, though his pallor—glistening fish-belly white— was a marked contrast to Barnes' ebony sheen. The man was shorter than Barnes, no more than five-five or -six, even counting the height of his tottering coiffure. He looked strong. That was the only possible word. His shoulders bulged beneath the brilliant green-and-blue print of his dashiki; the veins on the back of his thick hands swelled blue and prominent. He had a single golden eyebrow stretching from temple to temple and spreading halfway down the bridge of his patrician nose.

Kiley tensed his forearm to shake the man's hand, and seized a rubber glove full of lard. A cold bundle of fingers lay in his palm, dead. He dropped it.

"Hey, man. Whass happnin?" the redhead began. "Petah Clausewitz. Ah think y'already know Tom Barnes."

Kiley nodded. "How are you?"

"We gon in'duce you 'round, oney firs Ah'm a welcome you. We din git to rap none th'ovah day at the big meetin 'cause some Bizad mothahfuck done bus it up. Heah, it ain none them fuck wif us. You kin be relax, dig?"

"I've been relaxing. I'm about ready to go to work."

"Know what you mean, brother," Barnes said. "But lemme say sorry I got shook there in the hospital, the first time we talk." He glared at Jackie, obviously excluding her from his apology. "Sometime I let my temper run loose."

Clausewitz turned to face the expectant crowd. "Firs off, doan nobody ax no questions till we git done wif the presentation. If Mis' Kahley gon to feel to home heah, we gon have to do it raht. Mis' Kahley? Why not jus wave a han or somepin? We kin call that in'duction nuff and then let you know what we see comin the nex few weeks."

Kiley waved dutifully, exchanged smiles with the waiting Fac, who collectively leaned forward, poised like sprinters in the starting blocks. A chair nudged him behind the knees, and he dropped into it. Jackie patted his shoulder, pulled a second chair up beside him, and sat down.

"Raht on," Clausewitz said. "Ah'm a lay it out fas an clean. It's a plot go down everwhere 'round us, an you the one hep us git it togevah. Hallah, he lookin to git out of goin to Washinton wif the budget nex mumff, an we in a good way to pick who go in his place. Bes as Ah kin sum up, we all decide you gon go for us. The Senate ain 'bout to turn down no reques, it come from Robut Kahley hisself, way we figure. Wif you doin the talkin for us, ain no chance the Bizads git thoo to none them ofay sen'turs. An that mean we stomp on their plans to bring back that racis and sexis shit, an lack classscrimination 'gains ouah studenss." His voice rose with fervor to shout the final words. Applause sounded from a part of the crowd.

"You dig what he sayin there?" Barnes asked.

"I think so. Most of it. But understand, I'm not up on all the politicking that's going on. One of you could be a better spokesman—"

"Sheet, man! Ain none these mothahfuck got the clout you do. Anybody say so, he a lie."

"Can't you tell me what Bizads want? When I talked with them earlier, they didn't explain it very—"

"'Splain's ass! They ain let butter melt in they mouf, 'em mothahs. You yawn 'round 'at Bengston, he snatch the fillins raht outen youah teef. Ah tell you the firs thing they *ain* doin. They ain goin by *The Kahley 'posal* no more, an thass the truf." He looked to the audience and drew affirming nods.

"Is that enough to call it a plot?"

Clausewitz squinted, then donned his smile again. "Maybe not. Oney lemme give you th'eksential diffrence 'tween them an us. In whatevah they tole you, did you see studen one in theah wif 'em? No? You bet youah ass no! It's nuffin *lack* studen 'ticipation in what go down ovah theah. You take somepin lack one theah managemen courses. It's faculty plan it, teach it, and studenss ain say shit 'bout none of they own classwork. You talk 'bout youah eksential diffrence, 'at's it. They a bunch mealymouf facis, in which makin kids take courses ain relevan to nuffin in the worl. Sistah Mullah, she tell you."

Jackie nodded.

Kiley shrugged. They all seemed to agree. "Can you explain the budget to me? If I have to present it—"

"Now you talkin. Sure we kin. All you gotta know, we rap on it the nex few days. Then you keep a eye on Morgan, and see what shakin wif them sen'turs."

"Morgan, he the moneyman," Jackie whispered. "I'm explain later."

"Well. I'll do what I can," Kiley said. "I just hope you're not going to depend too much on me."

"Thass what we wanna heah." Clausewitz stirred up applause with his circling hands, then began to pace rapidly back and forth, his chin resting on his heavy chest while he glared at the floor and ranted. "But onlies thing Ah'm a have do in what tahm we got lef is clean up youah mouf. You go back to Washinton soundin lack some fuckin honky Bizad, they ain gon know wheah you at. So we figure three, four days intensive, maybe hypnotism an 'at shit, we fix up youah head."

"Pete?" A wizened Oriental woman near the front of the room stood to interrupt. "You really figurin to learn him everthing in a couple days? Half 'ese dudes ain talkin *real* black lack it is. Ah doan know how kin you ekspeck learn Mis' Kahley so fas." She peered at him through a skimpy fringe of gray bangs and plucked nervously at her flowing caftan.

"Then say, 'tween you *an* me. That what you wanna heah?"

She surveyed her seated colleagues. "Sure as shit ain nobody else kin do it. You heah so many kahns black anymoah, can't keep 'em straight."

Barnes thrust out his chin and shouted, "You tellin me you talks black better'n me? What the hell you—"

"If she doan, Ah do." Clausewitz threw his case to the audience. "Y'all heah what he say? You 'talks'?" He pantomimed amazement. "Wheah the fuck you fum, boy? Ain nobody 'cept southrun niggahs evah done that. You bin refresh lately? It's shit lack that in which give the Bizads what they usin 'gains us. It's all on the tapes, brothah. Even spoze you can't hannel the p'nunciation, git the fuckin grammah down, fore you go lecturin Sistah Chiu how to talk good."

He turned back to Kiley. "That Sistah Ling Chiu, theah. You work wif her, she do you raht. Ain but a few of us linguisis lack me an her lef in this whole place. If we ain keep the language pure, firs thing you know we all be back soundin lack Bizads." He spun on his heel and shouted, "That what y'all want?"

"No!" several answered.

"Then we agree? Sistah Chiu should work wif him?"

"Yes!" the same voices shouted.

"Y'all ready we give Mis' Kahley his s'prize?"

"YES!" The shout was unanimous, loudest from Jackie, who reached over to squeeze Kiley's hand.

He got no hint from her beaming smile, nor from the expectation graven on all the faces present. Whatever they had planned was a secret to no one, apparently, except him. Oddly, he thought of a bridal shower.

Sliding doors at the rear of the room split open and made him revise his analogy: a baby shower. Four tiny figures waddled into the room. At first glance they appeared nude. As they walked closer through the ringing applause he saw that they weren't really naked —each wore a pair of flesh-colored tights. Their feet were encased in blocks of milky translucent plastic. From crown to waist, each looked shaven and totally hairless.

And then he understood. They were living parodies of Robert Kiley, not of the Kiley who now sat hidden within his clothes but the Kiley whose pictures had filled the newspapers for days after his resurrection—Kiley naked on the operating table. He saw in them the appearance he must present to everyone he met. A final touch to their costumes recalled the actual moment of his waking. They weren't babies in diapers; each of them wore a bulky, stuffed, dangling, flaunted codpiece.

He blushed, and reddened with anger at feeling himself blush. "What's this about?" he whispered to Jackie.

"Mis' Kiley," one of the four piped in a childish tremulo. "We come to show you how proud we are to be at Urban U. Just like you."

He thought he heard femininity in the voice, though he couldn't be certain—it might be a boy. He stared at the codpiece she wore.

Barnes muttered, "Talk about somebody can't talk black. Goddamn dinge brat, think she can walk in here—"

"Go ahead!" Clausewitz shouted. "Finish it, else he think we put y'all up to it."

The girl took a nervous breath. "Pete here, he seen some of us goin to class and ask could we come meet you."

"Raht on. Ah'm doin little heel and toe, dig? Jus makin it easy ovah pas Chile Care, when Ah see a bunch them little mothahs out slidin round on those glass feet lack, an then Ah know. They all apin *you!* Make a man feel proud as shit, raht?"

Unable to speak, Kiley nodded.

"So Ah says to this chile, 'Honey. Just slide youah ass ovah to Fac lounge tonaht and let Mis' Kahley see foah hisself.' Who say 'ese little shit ain know what they want?"

The children stood in embarrassed silence, while titters circled the room and the adults cooed at their cuteness.

"Ask her what's her name," Jackie hissed.

Kiley brushed a nervous hand over his scalp and tried to focus only on the girl's eyes. He thought he detected the faintest swelling of her youthful breasts and wanted to embarrass neither her nor himself by staring. "Ummm. Uh—thank you. What, uh, what is your name?" He looked helplessly at Jackie.

"Susie Urban," the girl simpered. She made a circle of thumb and forefinger. Kiley misunderstood it as an "okay" sign, until she dropped her hand, flipped loose the forefinger, and snapped her codpiece.

Two of the other children made the same gesture.

Kiley watched his own hand start to move in response. He

managed to control it and jam the fist into his trouser pocket with only the slightest flinch. No one seemed to notice.

"Uh, well. Thank you, Susie. For, uh . . . for. . . . Thank you."

"Opensky," she said. "You gon be teachin a class or something?"

"Well, yes. I think so. But, uh . . . but I think it'll be for the older students. I mean—"

"Older's ass," one of the other hairless children snapped. "We all *seniors*, and it ain't likely no 'Mister' be teaching graduate class."

"Hush youah mouf, Willie," Clausewitz said. "Mis' Kahley teach what he fuckin well want to. Dig?"

After a moment of defiance in his stance, the boy nodded reluctantly. "You the boss, Pete." He looked as unrepentant as possible.

"It's a good point," Jackie said, rising to her feet for the first time. "Y'all heard 'em. He got the invitation, public and all. So does he get the class or not?" She motioned for Kiley to listen.

Kiley felt himself at one more of those crossroads he never seemed to recognize till he had passed them. A mutter rose but subsided quickly as everyone looked to Clausewitz for a decision.

"Why not? A studen pick you, you go 'head an teach. But less us wait an rap on that after. It's too much goin down ncx couple weeks for Mis' Kahley worry about classes and lack that." He dismissed the students with a wave, "Y'all go do what you do. It's good you come by, an we 'preciate it."

"What's that mean, ' 'preciate'? You givin us a fuckin 'A' or something?" Willie posed with hands on his hips.

"Don't get mouthy, boy!" Barnes strode toward him. "Maybe I fix it so you get one a them scholarships into Building and Grounds, dig?"

Muttering, Willie joined the other three children who had reached the back door. As he left, he whirled and gave his codpiece a snap in parting fillip.

"Kids," Clausewitz chuckled. "Same as when Ah was a boy. Can't learn 'em nuffin." He reached up to drape a meaty arm over

Kiley's shoulders. "Heah. Less meet some th'othahs." With careful contrivance he stepped between Kiley and Jackie. He pushed Kiley toward the waiting crowd.

"Later," Jackie called after him.

20

"LATER" turned out to be in Kiley's room. He collapsed into bed at three in the morning after a party he knew he would never forget but wasn't really sure he could remember. He had apparently acquitted himself well enough to impress Jackie. She joined him in his hospital bed at three-fifteen.

He did not acquit himself well there. He blamed it on the party. She blamed it on herself.

He fell asleep and dreamed of himself as Samson, castrated by a lady barber.

21

"Although Mr. Kiley's insight and intellect can hardly be doubted —the following pages offer ample testimony to that—his own academic record gives little hint of the man he was to become. It may be assumed that his interests in extracurricular activities kept him from devoting his full attention to the demands of the lecture hall."

Editors' Introduction, *The Kiley Proposal*

HE AWOKE at eight o'clock and found himself recovered from the depression of the early morning. A moment later, he found Jackie, a short arm's length away.

The rest of the morning contained little of novelty except for a few experiments with the adjustable bed itself.

When lunch arrived they were both too exhausted to chew. They toasted each other with bouillon, and napped.

22

"Can we afford to cower within our cozy studies while the needs of society cry out on every hand? We had better face the new world. Two choices loom before us: get out of the classroom and into the streets, or get out of the University."

The Kiley Proposal

FOR SEVERAL DAYS, Dr. Ling Chiu tutored Kiley in speaking black. She and Clausewitz were, as they claimed, the university's leading experts on the patois that had become the standard academic language. As a promising young graduate student, Ling Chiu had in fact helped gather data and codify rules for an official black grammar. Even before *The Kiley Proposal* appeared, she had begun her work; that gives her something in common with Kiley. They both represent a generation from the past. In his earlier life he might even have seen her, a shy student of twenty in her cheongsam and sandals, making her way across campus. He hadn't, as it turns out. But then neither has he thought to ask about survivors from his generation. She is the only one at Urban U.

Blame the shortened lifespan within the university—that, and the normal attrition of fifty-one years.

In her early seventies now, Ling Chiu was once younger than Kiley. And as eager. Armed with a tape recorder, she had stalked the ghetto surrounding the university and collected her data. It took several years; she is still a methodical woman. A computer accepted the data, analyzed and collated it. A computer-controlled linotype and press printed it. All in 1974. Once identified, so the language remained. Like members of *L'Académie Française*, she and Clausewitz defended the language against the corruption of time and against the permissiveness that had led many academics to ignore pronunciation and concentrate solely on grammar. That permissiveness infuriated her. She had been involved in the conception of the program, knew how perfect was the material collected, and could still recall the very faces of the ten blacks whose speech she had taped.

For several days running, she visited Kiley in his hospital room. She brought grammar casettes and what little printed material she could locate, then spent the mornings drilling him.

He was a slow learner. His lessons progressed; he didn't.

Dr. Chiu grew defensive and took to thinking dark thoughts about Kiley's intelligence. To do otherwise would call in question her skills as a teacher. Those were the two alternatives, she thought.

Another possibility completely escaped her. Kiley didn't want to learn. Had someone suggested that possibility to Dr. Chiu, she wouldn't have believed it. He was, after all, Robert Kiley. And no one suggested it. Least of all Kiley. He wasn't aware of it himself. All he knew was that he seemed to be having a problem.

He solved the problem. There is a nice irony in his solution: he solved it as most students had, though he didn't know that. His solution was simplicity itself. He stopped trying to learn. Not trying, he couldn't fail. Not failing, he could retain a sense of his own worth.

He said to Ling Chiu, "I don't think we ought to bother with this any more, do you?"

She agreed without question. How could she contradict Robert Kiley?

She left, feeling herself a failure. She was wrong. She hadn't taught him black, but—in a higher sense—neither had she failed. Her efforts had educated Robert Kiley. She taught him power.

She didn't know that. That afternoon she transferred five of her students to the Department of Buildings and Grounds, where they would spend their lives as Instructors of Maintenance, sweeping and cleaning. It helped to mitigate her failure. It restored her sense of power.

"Power" is the operative word.

Kiley felt relieved. He came to understand another facet of his personal authority. They couldn't deny him.

He flexed his reputation once more; and a squad of hospital personnel busied themselves in moving his few personal effects from his hospital room to Kiley House, on Kiley Avenue.

"I want to get out more," he explained to Jackie. "That's all."

She took it as a sign of his growing concern and was pleased. He seemed to be opening up. He wanted to get involved. She notified the Department of Child Care and moved to Kiley House with him. It was a definite step in the growth of Robert Kiley, evidence of Dr. Jacqueline Muller's effectiveness in leading him back into the world. Or into the university. To her, they were the same.

Her fondness for him grew.

23

"Too many of our assumptions are based on mere ancestor worship. 'Time makes ancient goods uncouth' is no less true now than when Holmes first said it. To respect the classics is one thing; to venerate the classicist quite another."

Preface, *The Kiley Proposal*

KILEY HOUSE is more a memorial than a home. The second-floor office Kiley had once shared with three other instructors is now a library that houses the many editions of his two books: *The Kiley Proposal* and *The Notebooks of Robert Kiley*, most of them containing pristine, uncut leaves. He will not recognize the place. The linoleum on the floor has been replaced by carpeting; fiberboard paneling covers the cracked plaster walls; there are drapes on the single window. The desk once shared by Kiley and Cooper Grimes has been bronzed (after a lengthy debate as to whether bronzing the whole desk, or only Kiley's half, was more appropriate). It reminds him of a dean's office. Or a chiropractor's.

The ground floor is a museum. It has been for years. As a visitor enters he is greeted by a hologram of Robert Kiley Himself (done from medical records and imagination), standing with each arm around the shoulders of a student: a white boy with red hair and freckles; a black girl with pigtails and a checked pinafore.

Beyond that insubstantial statue is row upon row of display cases containing artifacts. Shoes, pencils, a cup and saucer, a necktie, portable typewriter, coffee pot, driver's license, handball glove, and so on. As a visitor walks past the cases and breaks an electronic beam, each item is named by a recorded museum guide. On the faded red velvet cloth that lines each case is a small rectangle of bright scarlet. Several years earlier the Department of Records and Old Things will have removed from each case a small rectangular card that bore a printed description of the artifact on display.

They will do so, in fact, on the very day when they substitute an audiotape for the plaque on the cenotaph outside. The plaque that reads, HE BUILDED BETTER THAN HE KNEW.

When Kiley asked to leave the hospital, the curator of Kiley House was forced to move out of his third-floor apartment. He is Dr. Winston Nygaard, Chairman of the Department of Records and Old Things. He moved to the Urban Museum, whose curator was asked to move. . . . And so it went. Ninety-seven people in the Department of Records, etc. shifted jobs and domiciles, each moving one step downward in the pecking order. Kiley did not recognize how much upheaval his simple request would cause. Had he known when he made the request, he would have debated the move more carefully.

Three days earlier, he would not have moved.

Three days later, he would not have debated.

The day of his move occurs at a watershed in his development. It defines his power.

"Power" is the operative word.

24

"A final argument remains unanswerable. Our aim is to prepare students for adulthood. Maturation is marked by the ability to exercise free choice and to experience the sense of fulfillment which accompanies choosing correctly. We can give our students that fulfillment by terming 'correct' any choices they make."

The Kiley Proposal

MOVING to Kiley House did not free Kiley. It merely altered the shape of his restriction. He enjoyed two days of unofficial honeymoon. Then he endured two more days of the same honeymoon. He began to search his mind for excuses to get out of the house. It wasn't that he had lost interest in Jackie; during those random moments when he forgot about his new importance he actually felt affection for her, something possibly akin to love. But he had been drinking the antirect-treated water for some time now, and his ardor had become a thing of memory and performance-by-rote. When she began to forgive his incapacity he sought ways not to fail. He stopped trying.

It was easy to hide behind the excuse of exhaustion. Most of his (out-of-bed) waking hours were spent trying to memorize figures droned in his ear. Clausewitz sent tapes. Kiley listened to them. When he asked for a printed budget he was told that only Morgan had a copy.

And no one could describe Morgan, except to call him the moneyman.

Kiley's time wasn't wasted. Listening to budgets proposed for the several Fac programs, he began to understand the programs themselves. He tried matching his understanding to *The Kiley Proposal*, and occasionally succeeded. It all made him feel involved. He said so to Jackie. Unfortunately, his saying so made her affectionate. It was a real dilemma.

But Kiley was getting brighter. The daily injections of RNA and magnesium pemoline were working; his memory was returning; his thoughts became more direct, sharp, perceptive, day by day. Sitting near the tape deck, concentrating on one more recital of numbers and dates and man-hours and teaching load and facts and figures, he glanced up to see warmth in Jackie's smile. It gave him the shivers. The shivers gave him inspiration.

"Enough," he said. "How's chances of getting me some real clothes, instead of this thing?" He plucked at his gray coverall. Since his clothes hadn't survived his fifty-odd-year absence, he had nothing of his own to wear.

"Maybe we can collect some of the junk from those glass cases downstairs," he suggested.

Jackie's frown defined his suggestion as something between poor taste and sacrilege. "No. Let's us buy somethin new. I'm gon pick out somethin good for you."

They took one of the electric cabs parked at the curb and left it outside the six-block-square Department of Faculty Apparel. Kiley almost committed a *faux pas* by entering a doorway marked by a mosaic cap and gown, but Jackie stopped him in time and led him farther down the block. They passed through a high arch topped by a gilded statue of a man in full academic regalia—Ph.D. hood and all—the entrance appropriate to their rank.

Well, to Jackie's rank, and Kiley's eminence.

"Yes, doctors?" The clerk bowed them toward a fitting room, where Jackie picked out what she considered suitable and Kiley stood resigned and wary of the clerk's measuring hands.

Halfway through the ordeal he suddenly realized, "I don't have any money."

"What you think been payin the freight up to now?" Jackie drew a small golden card from her pocket and waved it. "They got you on a special account. Did you think I was keepin you or somethin?"

The clerk glanced at the card and went pale. "But that's only for—" He stared at Kiley and jerked his hands away as if burned.

Jackie caught him as he fainted.

"You and Morgan," she said, "is the only ones got carte blanche."

Kiley helped the clerk to a chair. Fluttering eyelids rewarded him, and kept fluttering for the next ten minutes.

They left assured that the packages would be delivered.

"Probably beat us home," Jackie said. "Was I to go buyin somethin on my card, they likely cut me off in a couple days, the way you livin."

"Really carte blanche? Not a salary, you mean?"

"It ain't nobody get a salary no more. You just buys what you want till they say 'Stop.' Then you waits till next month."

"But how do you know how much—"

"Don't. They tells you. Does it matter?"

In a peculiar way, it did. Not that he was mercenary, but salary mattered. "That's how you keep score, isn't it? You get so much a month, Bengston gets so much, I get so much. Doesn't salary correspond to rank? When you get promoted, there must be a raise along with it."

Jackie laughed. "Maybe that why I'm a have such a good time 'round you. You got some the funniest ideas I ever heard. If you gets all you need to eat and like that, what you want more for?"

"Okay. Only *someone* must know what I'm worth to the university."

She waved the gold card again.

He took that as an answer. Everyone hears what he wants to hear.

25

"The Committee requests immediate access to the University budget and the election (from among faculty and students) of a permanent Finance Committee empowered to modify financial arrangements in line with the new programs described herein."

The Kiley Proposal

"Today [I] sat through a reading of the new budget. [The presentation was] so full of economic jargon [that some listeners] couldn't make any sense of it."

The Notebooks of Robert Kiley
(as edited)

MORGAN KNOWS what Kiley is worth to the university. Morgan knows everything. If a sparrow were to fall anywhere on campus, Morgan would know. There are no living sparrows within the university forcefield dome, of course, but the principle still holds: Morgan knows to the second decimal point how many rats will die on any given day, the average annual rainfall allowed to dampen the grass in University Park, the number of after-dinner mints likely to be consumed by the entire university population every day (Saturday is the biggest mint day). Morgan knows everything. And not only statistically, which is a false kind of knowledge. Of course Morgan knows statistics; more than that, Morgan knows actual numbers. That is why he is Morgan.

Everyone at Urban U. knows of Morgan, but many think he is a computer. They are essentially wrong. Morgan is soft, malleable, filled with the gurgling and swishing that sounds within any bag of living meat. Morgan is a man. Perhaps Morgan is also a computer, but a definition like that must be metaphorical. Call him an organic computer, if you like. Morgan runs the university.

Very few people in the university have ever seen Morgan, and their descriptions would not tally, should they ever think to compare

notes. They don't. No one discusses Morgan. Instead, people generally leave —— in their conversation when his post, or position,
or authority is implied.

Bengston would describe Morgan as a loud man. He had
spoken with him several times, usually to accept criticism of the
grandiose (and therefore expensive) plans conceived by the Department of Business Administration.

Clausewitz would describe Morgan as a tall man, because all
men are taller than Clausewitz, to his mind. In his mind he carries
a syllogism: "All men are taller than me; Morgan is taller than me;
therefore Morgan is a man." Clausewitz's mental disorder is not
our concern; those are his thoughts.

President Philip J. Haller would describe Morgan as a busy man.
Any time Haller wanted to see Morgan, to discuss questions carefully dinned into Haller's leaky memory by Facrep or Bizad lobbyists,
Morgan was busy. Twice Haller had spoken to Morgan face-to-
face. Once on the way to Washington to submit last year's budget
request; once on the way back to Urban U. with the approved request. On the way to Washington, Morgan had seemed over six feet
tall, with blue eyes, blond hair, ruddy complexion, and a store of
bawdy jokes. On the way home from Washington, Morgan had
seemed dark, sullen, short, dirty, balding, and uncommunicative.
Haller supposed such discrepancies were caused by being busy. He
couldn't be certain; he was never busy himself. And he was happy
for that. It did strange things to Morgan.

To be "Morgan" at Urban University—or at any university in
the land, for that matter—was not Nirvana. Each budget term,
Washington sends to each university a different Morgan, generally
a man eager to get ahead in the National Bureau of Budget Control
and therefore willing to endure his term within the confines of a
university forcefield dome. That is one way a man might gain pre-
ferment. Accepting such a post proves commitment to matters of
national concern and has made careers for scores of minor bureau-
crats.

There is a pattern to being Morgan. Taking the approved fund authorization to the university, Morgan is always sullen and unhappy; returning to Washington a year later with requests for the following academic term, Morgan is always jovial, ebullient, outgoing, happy, cheerful, delighted, elated, and so on.

No one really wants to *be* Morgan—named, of course, for the legendary financier—but everyone (outside the university) would dearly love to *have been* Morgan.

Morgan knows what Robert Kiley is worth to Urban University: $1,617,588.27 to date—research, recovery, and hospital costs comprising most of that figure. What little Kiley could eat, or drink, or wear, or in any way use was scarcely worth accounting for, now that the major expense had passed. Still, Morgan kept perfect count of those minor expenses as well. So that's what Kiley is worth, if costs describe worth. To Morgan they do.

Beyond that, Kiley has another worth: Kiley has a worth to Morgan. By taking Kiley to Washington with him this year, Morgan hopes to be promoted from GS 22 to GS 30. All ex-Morgans move to GS 25, but no other Morgan ever had in tow the man responsible for it all, the theoretician on whose philosophy (which Morgan had never read or listened to) the system had been founded. He plans to bask in the glory reflected from Kiley.

As Kiley steps from the Department of Faculty Apparel into the street, Morgan watches Kiley's purchase register in the special account clattering and clicking its numbers under his transparent desktop. And Morgan, this Morgan—whose real name is, unfortunately for his political ambitions, Harold Stassen—the Morgan of Urban University gloats as the numbers mount higher. No one will be able to accuse him of thwarting Robert Kiley in any way. He and Robert Kiley will go to Washington together.

But only Robert Kiley will return.

Morgan knows what Robert Kiley is worth.

26

"[Although] some of these students' demands are plain crazy
[. . . sentence apparently never finished]."

The Notebooks of Robert Kiley
(as edited)

As MORGAN WATCHES Kiley's purchase register in the special
account clattering and clicking its numbers under his transparent
desktop, Kiley steps from the Department of Faculty Apparel into
the street. He and Jackie stroll to the nearest cabstand and enter an
electric cab. She inserts Kiley's gold card into the dashboard slot.
The counter in Morgan's office registers again. Morgan knows what
Kiley is about. The cab thrums to life. To this point, everything is
normal.

Only then did Kiley notice the face peering in at him through
the side window—a young, black face, downy-cheeked, bright of eye,
innocent. It was a boy who motioned to him. Something wrong
with the cab.

Kiley acted out of character. The old Kiley would have hesitated uncertainly; the new Kiley hesitated not at all. He depressed
a stud, and the window slipped silently down into the door.

"Wha—" he started to ask.

Something stung his neck, and he felt his tongue swell to fill
his mouth. Before unconsciousness took him he saw the boy's hand
swimming away through a pink haze into darkness. In the hand,
what looked like a Ping-Pong ball. He knew that couldn't be right.

Mentally, he lunged toward the boy to fend him off. Physically,
his right arm twitched and he uttered a soft "Hunnnnh."

27

URBAN UNIVERSITY is circular. For reasons known only to five theoretical physicists in the world, a forcefield shell must be circular at the base. It has something to do with the dome effect. The explanation lies in mathematics, not in words, but you will be able to look it up. If you like. If you can understand it.

The several ranks of buildings nearest the crackling mist-green shell are termed "Workring" in the local slang. All the manufacturing departments of the university are located in Workring. They have easy access to exit points. Raw materials enter through those guarded ports; manufactured goods exit. It is most efficient.

Only the students and faculty assigned to those departments dislike the location, for reasons having nothing to do with the education offered there. They dislike the noise and the smell. Not the noise of the factories themselves, but the noise of the air ducts.

For, every hundred yards along the curved base of the forcefield shell, there is an intake that inhales the filth of the atmosphere within the university. Air, dust, wind-blown debris, and careless small animals are drawn into the howling ducts, which roar like hundreds of Hoovers. The air is cleansed, purified, humidified, and released once more, nearly breathable, at the center of the university. Two blocks from Kiley House, in fact, in University Park. Its emission is silent. No one minds that.

It rises above the buildings at university center and begins its arcing return to the ducts. On the way, it accumulates sulfur, nitrous oxides, bits of carbon ash—all the effluvia of any industrial complex. By the time a cubic foot of purified air returns unpurified to the ducts, it contains one ounce of airborne crud and has developed a distinct character. The students who brush that air out of their eyes every day have a definition. They say it's strong enough to gag a maggot.

It does have a tangible aroma. As the finest French perfume is to excrement, so is excrement to the air settling over Workring.

Kiley would not draw such an analogy. When he regained consciousness inside one of the massive intake ducts, he thought he smelled a burned palomino. Distorted shapes and shadows drifted along a curving metal wall beside him. His ears popped as the air pressure swelled and diminished. Then the metal wall was moving back over his head. A tinny clatter sounded through the roar of wind like a distant tambourine.

Slowly, he focused his senses.

The wall wasn't moving, he was. Before him, hoisted into view, were his own legs—no mistaking those prosthetic clogs. Tiny hands clasped each ankle and pulled him along. He lay on his back, Gulliver on a small wheeled platform, and was towed through the roar of the dark tornado. The platform casters clattered beneath his head.

Suddenly the ceiling leaped away, lights flared, and the wind died like a muted droning organ. Light breezes played over him, still redolent of roasted horse. Before he could sit erect, a squeaking voice called out, "Mister Kiley? Want to get up now? The headache won't last long."

He smiled to himself, proportion restored. He didn't *have* a headache. He rolled onto his side to rise, and a chorus of jackhammers began playing street-repair tunes behind his eyes.

"Here. Let me help. It won't be but a minute."

Hands dragged him erect. His pain faded and passed. And he could see. "This is the damndest place! Why can't I *walk* where I'm going?" He scanned the huge stone room and looked for authority, someone to answer his anger. He thought of catacombs. Fieldstone and masonry walls stretched away at both sides beneath a vaulted ceiling. He glanced over his shoulder to see a bulky curtain fluttering in the doorway he had been dragged through. A circle of faces stared at him. Neutral, waiting faces, some black, some white. None of them more than twelve or thirteen, or so it seemed. A kiddie brigade, all dressed in the gray coverall of the Department of Buildings and Grounds. He recalled fraternity initiations, scavenger hunts, all the childish games that might involve his capture; yet a feeling of tension in the fetid air denied each suggestion he offered himself. One of the black children pointed a small bronze tube in his direction. "Eversharp," Kiley mumbled, but instantly knew it was a weapon. Eversharp sounded archaic in this setting, even to him.

"Headache gone?"

"Eversharp."

"What?"

Kiley smiled. Let them be as confused as he was. He felt ludicrous, standing here at pen-point before a bunch of children. All children.

"Where's Doctor Muller?" he asked.

"She's opensky. Not to worry."

The tone of the answer satisfied him. It sounded reassuring without making sense. "You didn't want her here?"

"We didn't want *you* here," a girl said. "But we don't vote much any more."

The boy with the pen motioned her silent, while Kiley looked more closely to discover how he had recognized sex. In most cases not by figure; they all looked like boy gymnasts. Something else, something indefinable in their features separated his captors. Seven girls, nine boys, he counted. Sixteen in all. Twelve black.

"Some of us thought we ought to give you a chance to talk, before—"

The omitted promise didn't sound like a testimonial.

They were all watching him too closely for that. Kiley had the hunch that, after several days of calm, he had wandered outside the eye of the hurricane.

As if reading his mind, the pen wielder said, "You're an important man. The way you lean tips lots of other people. If it was up to the others, they'd say dump on you, but I get the feeling you're not as stupid as they think."

"I've been more flattered."

"Flattered's right. Part of it's because you're visible. Fac and

Bizads don't give a rat's ass about you, any more than they do about us. It's a game they're playing."

"He knows that," the same girl interrupted. "Get on with it."

"I agree. Say it and get finished. I can't hang around—"

A thin shaft of light from the Eversharp touched his right foot. He watched in amazement as the front of the clog softened, and melted, and ran to the floor. "Now what was—?" Fire interrupted him. Lava seared the toes that weren't there, and agony gnawed its way up his leg. He tried to hop on the good foot but collapsed to the floor writhing, until a boy poured a pail of water over the melting clog. The pail had been waiting, ready. Through the tears in his eyes he saw several more buckets, ranked in the shadows along the wall. He lay still and waited. It might be a long afternoon.

Slowly the throbbing subsided.

They were all smiling.

"Still think it's a party we asked you to?" The boy waved his weapon and gloated.

"Who are you?" Kiley hated the whine he heard in his voice.

"No names, Mister Kiley. It's enough that we know who you are. Call us 'dropouts.' That's a word you used in your books, isn't it? And don't figure these uniforms identify us. They're neutral, right? Nobody ever sees a nigger's face. He's an 'instructor of maintenance,' or 'one of them.' You're polite to him, but you don't see him. Well, nobody sees us, in these coveralls. Simple, isn't it?"

The comments sounded programmed. Kiley tried racing ahead of the oration he could sense coming—gripes, of some sort, marshaled into a philosophy. Urban U. apparently had its disenchanted. They didn't look much different from the few students he had already seen, except that they clearly weren't Kiley worshipers.

"What do you want with me?"

"Just some attention." The boy flicked on his weapon and scored a line on the floor beside Kiley's hand.

"You're crazy!" Kiley snatched his hand away from the heat. "Okay. Talk. But keep that thing to yourself."

"It's an old trick," the girl said. "You can teach 'em anything, but first you got to get their attention, ain't so?"

The leader walked down the tunnel away from the windy entrance, and Kiley followed, limping carefully between the files of children, who drew aside to let him pass. They fell in behind as escort. At a turn in the tunnel they reached an alcove in the stone wall. Several crates stood as seats, a blackboard hung on the wall, and a handful of books and scattered papers lay atop an upended barrel near the blackboard.

"Maybe it's not much, Kiley. But this is where you ought to think about holding that class you want to teach. I said you could call us dropouts. Maybe drop*ins* is better. In terms you can understand, we're the counter-U."

Filled with the short, slender figures of his guards, the alcove seemed a clubhouse. Kiley fought the smile that started to form; it wasn't a game to these kids, no matter what he thought. His leg still hurt.

"You know enough about my plans. Why not wait till I start teaching? As I understand it, anyone can drop in on any class."

"Get off that garbage, boy!" The angry white girl poked a finger into Kiley's chest. He wanted to say "Stop, I'll buy your cookies," but hesitated.

He was becoming the old Kiley again.

"We don't give a ruddy rat's ass *what* you teach, or when, or even where." Her eyes were pale blue in closeup, with only a pinprick of pupil. She leaned even closer. "All we want is people to know you're with *us*, not with anybody else. You don't have anything in your head I want to know. Let's start there. If they weren't feeding you like a pet, you'd starve. All we want is the halo you're wearing. Stay with us, let them know whose side you're on, and maybe we can make some changes.

"Tyrone's too damn nervous to squat, so I'll make it plain. We're coming through, Kiley. With you or without you. Anybody on the wrong side when the crunch starts gets dumped on. Down the ducts. Got it?"

He stepped back from her vehemence and nodded. "Okay. A revolution, right? You take over and change the world. But what you want is a volunteer, not someone drafted. How do I agree when I don't understand?"

"Miss Tricia Mouthy here is kind of free with names," Tyrone said, taking command again. "But maybe she's right. You want a program laid out? Here it is. We scrap that ratty *Kiley Proposal*. . . ."

"Hey!" the watching children chanted.

"We let you know what classes we'll have."

"Hey!"

"The forcefield comes down."

"Hey!" *Clap.*

"Free travel into opensky."

"Hey!" *Clap.*

"We pick the departments we work in."

"Hey!" *Clap.*

"And Retardo's OUT!"

"HEY!" *Applause.*

Kiley felt like a metronome, his head swinging in rhythm from Tyrone to the children chanting their litany. They laughed and chattered among themselves, all but Tyrone and the angry girl, who peered at him seeking reaction.

Foolishly, the new Kiley blurted, "Who put you up to this? You kids didn't come up with—"

The laser beam brushed his new coat sleeve, and he slapped at the smoldering tweed.

"And that kind of assumption gets ratted, too. 'Kids' ain't a word any more, Kiley. That's cloudmouth we don't listen to, understand?" Tyrone handed him a card.

The gesture seemed so formal, a textbook salesman about to present his wares, that Kiley didn't focus on the card at first. When he did, he saw a caricature of himself, reclining, tumescent, and a pair of children holding hands. On the back of the card were printed block capitals that spelled: OUT RETARDO. GET A KILEY.

He thought *coke*. The transition from proper name to generic term marks real fame, Coke to coke. "Kiley" looked headed in that same direction: from proper name to euphemism. He didn't like it. The distinction between fame and notoriety is a small one.

"See it?" the girl asked. "A woman can be castrated, too."

"Not because of *me*. I never *heard* of this drug you all keep griping about. Why am I the villain?"

Tyrone snatched a book off the upended barrel and flipped through it. In a moment, triumphant, he read, ". . . 'to prolong a student's term in school is regarded by some as a thinly disguised means of reducing the potential labor force. So long as any student, no matter his age, is defined as a child, he represents no competitive threat to those who pay for his holiday from adult responsibility.' Okay? Who says it clearer?"

"But you don't under—"

"There's more. A footnote: 'Recent research into steroid hormones such as estrone ($C_{18}H_{22}O_2$) reveals an interesting possibility. Orally ingested estrogens not only preclude conception; a variant of commercially available progesterone ($C_{21}H_{30}O_2$) has proven effective in retarding the onset of puberty. The implications for the academic community are myriad.'

"Well, myriad's rat! It comes down to Retardo—keep 'em in their place. And we're done with it."

The boy handed the book to Kiley, who didn't have to check the spine. He knew the title.

"'Footnote,' you said. You know I didn't write that. How am I responsible for—"

"*Why* do we know that?"

"Because I'm *telling* you so. Am I to blame for whatever someone else says in my name?"

"Uh-huh."

"HEY!"

The children surrounded him.

He saw sympathy in none of their faces. Nothing he could say would persuade them that he wasn't somehow "the enemy." He said nothing.

They began again.

For two hours Kiley listened to a verbal crucifixion of the man he had never been. No matter his explanations, or excuses, or pleas, they returned to one answer. They held out his book and thumped it. Periodically, Tyrone or the girl, Tricia, stepped out of earshot to caucus with his other captors, then returned to the attack. When it became obvious that he couldn't reason with them, couldn't show them how foolish they were to believe differently from him, he gave in.

"Maybe you're right. I don't know what you think I can do about it all, but let me think it all over. Then—"

"Not too long, boy," the girl said. "And sure not till you sic Security on us. We'll be around. The first time we hear you sounding like Kiley, we'll see you again."

"Fair enough. Now—"

"You don't get it. I didn't say you'd see *us*. Personally, I think we're wasting time on you. But some of the others want it this way, so we'll try you. No more conversations. When you see what we're saying, we'll know. Let's say, next week."

"What, 'next week'?"

"You straighten out your ideas, decide to join us and help the way you can, and all opensky. If not, start looking over your shoulder."

"Next week, Friday," Tyrone said. He held out a hand.

Instinctively, Kiley reached to shake it. The hand slapped him on the neck.

He had time to understand the stinging sensation before he blacked out. Mentally, he shrugged in resignation. Physically, he winked.

28

TYRONE FLOY SLUMPED when he walked. It made him appear shorter than his actual height. Unfortunately, it made him look nearly as old as his actual age. Problems like that confused him. He already had enough hanging over his head. His father had dropped hints about excessive absence from hygiene class. Rather than resort to useless arguments with the old man, Tyrone had begun to attend more faithfully than ever. Each day he climbed the steps to his father's office, accepted his Retardo, palmed it, and swallowed a bit of water. His father was content; no one had to know.

As he left the building each day, Tyrone poked the Retardo capsule into the soft dirt of the doorstep flowerbox. Two plastic geraniums stood in that box. Since Tyrone had begun to dose them with Retardo, neither had grown an inch. They had not grown before that, either, but Tyrone hadn't been responsible then. He was responsible only for their recent lack of growth. It was his own small joke. Only a child would understand it.

And only a bright child, at that. Tyrone was bright. Perhaps even brilliant. Self-educated, determined, cautious, and devious like any revolutionary, he also carried the broad banner of fanaticism. A fanatic in the right cause becomes a culture hero, a patriot. The jury was still out on Tyrone's cause. But not for long. Kiley represented a lever that the right man could use to move the world.

Tyrone tried to reassure himself. In the presence of his fellow conspirators he seemed certain. He carried the laser, he made the decisions, he was the leader. But in private he harbored the sort of uncertainty that can ruin any leader when the moment of crisis arrives. Though he knew he was no longer a child, his body was slow to get the message. His presexuality troubled him in the deepest recesses of his mind. Only that shortcoming stood between him and total certitude.

He recalled Kiley's accidental wink and shuddered. It was as if Kiley had seen the truth about him. He wasn't yet a man.

For the fourth time that week, Tyrone ducked into the student lounge and headed for the Boys' Room.

29

TWO SECURITY GUARDS patrolling campus center found Kiley propped against the side of the building where Carleton Floy had his office. He lay with his head between two plastic geraniums in the flowerbox and wheezed noisily enough to draw their attention. At first they thought he was a student, given his baldness and square ceramic shoes. A closer look identified him as the original, not an imitation. There are not many like Kiley lying around.

They carried him across the street to Kiley House, where Jackie persuaded them not to report their discovery.

Hers was the first face he saw when he awoke. He expected it.

"What happened to you?" he croaked. He knew better than to move suddenly, and lay waiting for the headache to strike and withdraw.

"Tranquilizers, far as I know. When I come to I was sittin in the cab where you left me."

"I left you? A bunch of Munchkins carried me off into some dungeon and started roasting my toes." He pointed to the scarred clog. "The Spanish Inquisition, all over again. All I had to do was convert to their version of truth and they let me go."

"D'you mean students done that? It ain't none of them don't love you like a mother."

He flinched at some recent embarrassment. "Can't you say 'father'? Besides, you're wrong. At first I thought it was a game, Cub Scouts trying to be funny, but it didn't turn out that way. They called themselves the 'counter-U.' Does that mean anything to you?"

"What's a Cub Scout?"

"They recited a list of gripes and expected me to wave my wand and set the world right. I don't even know where they took me. Some place windy, full of tunnels. Smelled like a garbage dump."

"Likely they hidin in the air ducts again." Jackie strolled over to the nightstand and began to brush her hair. The whole affair obviously meant little to her.

Irritated, he watched the brush slashing rhythmic static through her boyish curls and waited for her attention.

Finally, he snapped, "Are you listening?"

"Uh-huh. But it ain't nuthin we can do 'bout it. You come back safe. No harm done, and—"

"What about this?" He lay back on the bed and hoisted his damaged clog.

"Them kids." She shook her head in cryptic admiration. "Sometime they does the silliest things. In the morning we go fix you up. But you gon have to learn to stay away from 'em." She shook a warning finger. "It ain't do you no good, did people think you gettin hook up with somebody like that."

He stormed over to grab her shoulder and spin her around. "Who are they? You talk as if I know all about them, and I'm telling you they meant business. They even gave me a deadline. By next Friday I'm supposed to do something, or *be* something, to satisfy them. Otherwise they'll haul me off to their fortress again. Now this is serious, dammit!"

She patted his cheek with one hand while the other kept the hairbrush in motion. "'Serious' ass, man. They only playin, like kids always does. No matter what we does for them, they wants somethin else. I make it you got carry off by some the students ain't doin so good in school, 'sall. They got to have some way to let off steam. Mostly they hides in the air ducts. Once in a while they comes out and sets fires, or either starts snipin at some teacher, but they—"

"Oh. That's okay, then. I got it. Set a few fires, shoot a few people. Fine. Right. I understand. Nothing serious. A few fires. . . ." He shook his head and collapsed into a chair. Clearly he and Jackie weren't talking about the same thing. And more clearly, she had no real concern for him, didn't care a bit about his problems. He sat sulking.

When his silence registered, she laid down her brush and walked over to rest a comforting hand on his bald scalp. "I'm sorry. Probably it do be sort of shockin, bein how it's strange to you and all. But fires ain't much, if you think on it. We just rebuilds. And you can't say that's new for you. You was havin fires when you was here before. Right? Far as snipin go. . . ." She ran a cool hand inside his collar and patted his scars.

"Just don't pay 'em no attention. We got more important things to do, anyway. Bengston, he call an hour ago. He got some silly idea you gon work with him on his own budget stuff. Maybe it's best you call him back. Sooner everyone know you stickin with Fac, where you belongs, sooner all these peoples stop screwin with you. You call him, or either I call him for you, one."

"Uh-huh. I make a public announcement, is that it? 'Robert Kiley has taken a position with X.' Well, those kids won't take an answer like that. As soon as I stick my neck out, they're waiting to lop off my head.

"Listen. Is there any chance I can hire some protection? Maybe a bodyguard?"

She paled and jerked away as if bitten. Whatever he had said had struck a nerve. Softly, she asked, "Ain't I been doin right by you?" Tears glimmered in her eyes, and she turned away to hide them.

"Now wait. Are we talking about the same thing? I said 'bodyguard,' and you react like this. I don't make the connection."

Sniffing, she mumbled, "It's *me* takin care of you." She looked at him as though he sat dismembering her favorite cat. "If I ain't do it right, say so, and maybe someone else come do it. Whatever you wants."

"It's not that way." He pulled her onto his lap, cupped a hand under her chin, and made her face him. "I *deserve* protection, don't I? I never asked for any of this. People are pulling me nine ways from Sunday. Everyone wants a piece of my life, and most of it involves things I can't control. I don't even *understand*. Besides all that, there's no one I want here but you." He raised her chin to kiss her, but she resisted.

"You ain't up to 'at shit now. We got stuff to settle here."

He pushed her away. "Great! Wonderful! That's the way to cool a guy down." He stood and began to pace. "If I behave, everything's fine. If I don't play your way, it's sleep on the couch. Right?"

Her eyes answered first. She stood on the balls of her feet, poised like a stalking cat, and faced him down. "*That's* what you think of me! There's a word for a woman like that. Want to say it out loud, or should I?"

This time he refused to bend. Like an angry ballplayer fronting an umpire, he leaned into her anger till their noses nearly touched. "What happened to the dialect?"

"Okay, *racist*. Change the subject. That's your way out. Do you think it's easy for me to talk black? I wasn't raised with it. I had to learn it, the same way you could. *Could*, I said. If you wanted to. But that would be work, wouldn't it? And you're happy living off the rest of us. When do you start carrying your own weight around here? You think I've got nothing to do but nursemaid your ego? Should I—"

"Hold it!" He backed her away with his vehemence. "Let's start with 'racist.' Today I talked with some black kids, and they sounded nothing like you. And less than nothing like Clausewitz. You're spouting a dialect that's years out of date. Sure, you can teach someone to use it, but why? Priests used to speak Latin. What's the point? Nobody I've seen here talks black except a handful of patronizing bigots. You said we had the burning in my day. We also had people who wanted to 'meet the students at their own level.' Direct quotation: I saw it in some idiot's footnote to my book.

"No, wait. Don't turn your back on me. Reach them on their own level. That assumes '*they*' can't learn anything but what they already know. Pat 'em on the head and walk away. If I ever heard bigotry and patronizing, that's it. Not me. *You!*"

The silence was painful. Both knew they had said too much.

Neither could back down. Though Kiley framed an apology, it stuck in his throat.

Jackie turned and began methodically to strip her clothes from the wardrobe racks.

Kiley watched her.

She walked out stiff-legged and returned for another armload.

He knew it wasn't fair, blaming her for all the tension and uncertainty he felt. He tried to be fair.

"Okay. Look. Let's skip all that. You said 'carry my own weight.' I agree. I've been saying the same thing all along. What do I know about all this political maneuvering? I'm a teacher. If you still want to help, get me a classroom."

Still not looking at him, she sat on the edge of the bed, head bowed, hands folded in her lap.

"Thank you. That's better. Now. When does the next term begin?"

"It ain't . . . there aren't any terms the way you mean it. When a student asks you to teach, you teach. Start any time."

"Make it Monday. Is that too soon?"

She shook her head.

"All right. Monday. If you want a title for the class, call it 'American Idealism.' "

Now she looked at him. To stare in bewilderment. "But—"

"Well?"

She turned away.

"Monday?"

"Yes sir."

"There's no need for—"

"YES SIR!" She flounced from the room. Then her voice drifted back with the last word. "And it's *me* gon sleep on the fuckin couch!"

He opened his mouth to shout but choked helplessly. He spun angrily and looked for something to throw. When nothing came to hand, he lashed out and kicked a wooden chair. The chair leg splintered, and he stared amazed at the wreckage, till he remembered his solid glass foot.

From somewhere he drew enough strength for a bitter smile.

30

"Last night [I] saw a student production of *Hamlet* [performed by an] all-nude cast. [The production provided] a new rationale for Hamlet's hesitation—nobody's a hero in his birthday suit."

The Notebooks of Robert Kiley
(as edited)

THERE IS MUCH to be said about quarreling, not all of it negative. Creative quarreling can sometimes define a relationship better than the best-intentioned acquiescence. Like infantrymen in battle, ideas and opinions are best tested under fire. On the other hand, quarreling always leads to unintended exaggerations, and they can hurt a sensitive soul.

Jackie Muller is sensitive.

Kiley thinks he is, too. He's wrong, but who will tell him so? Everyone around him takes great pains not to contradict Robert Kiley. He is the emperor in new clothes.

That's only one of his problems. Most of the others can be lumped as one: he has too many choices. During the sleepless hours following his quarrel with Jackie, he will lie awake and weigh the merits and shortcomings of each choice. As well as he can. Given what he knows.

He might choose to support the Bizads, although to his slightly effete tastes they seem crude machinators. And Bengston's voice makes his fillings ache. The Bizads unfortunately regard everyone as grist for their experimental mills. On the other hand, they *are* teaching something to someone.

Fac, so far as Kiley knows, are teaching nothing to anyone. So far as he knows. On the other hand, they do treat their students nearly as equals, at times, and as human beings, at other times.

The disenchanted students, the counter-U group, are radical malcontents. On the other hand—there is always one of those—on the other hand, the very thought of drugged and demeaned children is repugnant to Kiley's every ideal. *The Kiley Proposal*, no matter its final effect, had been born in idealism. Spoiled idealism stinks worse than burned palomino.

Those are the choices Kiley is consciously aware of. Another choice lies deeply hidden within him, suppressed, held beneath consciousness by the weight of his newfound satisfactions. He might repudiate *The Kiley Proposal* entirely. He might give up his eminence. He might remove himself from the halls of power. That he won't do. Very few would.

And there are other choices, of which Kiley knows little or nothing. Morgan would use him. Jackie has been using him, though in a noble rather than a self-serving way. And so on. And so on.

Anyone would be edgy under such circumstances. Anyone might be quick to anger and willing to say things he didn't entirely mean. Anyone is likely to run for the best cover available. A classroom is Kiley's hiding place. He is a good teacher. He can run toward that fact as security. It will help restore his certitude; it will help postpone those difficult decisions. It will allow him to wait.

31

"Promotions should depend exclusively upon student evaluation of teaching aptitude and performance."

The Kiley Proposal

IN A CLOSED COMMUNITY, news travels with amazing speed. On Saturday morning, Jackie reserved a classroom for Kiley's Monday use. By noon the same day news media were already celebrating the event.

Newshawks on all three U-net trivee stations spoke of little else.

The pictographic *News* devoted all four pages of its noon edition to drawings of Kiley's plans. He was easy to recognize; his plans weren't. The drawings showed actions, not motives, of course. They could not communicate every nuance of the situation. The concept "idealism" is beyond any cartoonist's skill to depict.

People too busy to struggle through the pictographic series in the *News* learned of the excitement when they picked up an *Infocap* extra from streetcorner hawkers. That afternoon subway trains were filled with the crackling information as each commuter pulled the string on his *Infocap* and listened to the crisp static recording.

Even the conservative, small-circulation *Times* devoted two of its ten printed pages to the forthcoming event—in parallel columns of oldspeak prose (for students and semiliterates) and stewartalk (for Faculty).

(Dr. Ling Chiu had long since abandoned her campaign to have stewartalk renamed Lingo. Though her local reputation was secure, she lacked the national stature of Stewart himself, the man who had years before temporarily revolutionized the now-moribund textbook industry with his simple idea of rewriting "The Night Before Christmas" in black English. Though academese might be Lingo to Dr. Chiu, in the popular mind it remained stewartalk.)

According to the *Times*:

On Monday, December 14, Mr. Robert Kiley will begin a series of public lectures to be titled "American Idealism." His first lecture is scheduled for 10 A.M. in the newly completed Borgward Hall auditorium (see side bar). Attendance will be restricted to Students and Faculty in the Department of Humanities. Others may attend by invitation only.

All three university trivee

Mr. Robert Kiley going to give a talk next Monday. He will talk many times after. He will talk in the new Borgward Hall (Borgward Hall describe in square box on this page). It's all Humanity students and teachers can go hear him. Other peoples is ask to stay away without they get ask to go.

Trivee stations going to show Kiley talk. They will cancel regular shows. Dr. Rudnick, he networks plan live coverage of the entire series and will cancel regular programming. Dr. J. Cameron Rudnick, Director of U. Broadcast Media, said, "Of course we will. Our networks have an obligation to carry programs of current public interest. Most of our viewers will understand the need for this change in programming."

Mr. Kiley was unavailable for comment, but Dr. Jacqueline Muller. . . .

head of Broadcasting, he say, "No jive. We-all's stations have to show what going down now. It's most peoples watching dig what we doing be right."

Mr. Kiley, he ain't around to answer questions his own self, so Dr. Jacqueline Muller, she say. . . .

With all the excitement in the air, Morgan began to fear for Kiley's safety. He pushed appropriate buttons, and someone in the Department of Security decided to supplement the normal quota of four guards per classroom. Students were enlisted from the unemployed in the Department of Buildings and Grounds. Tyrone Floy joined the group.

Only Kiley missed the excitement, shielded from it by Jackie's solicitude and by his own abstraction. After a glazier repaired his damaged foot, he grew so busy planning his lecture that he felt himself almost at home again. He sat at the bronzed desk on the second floor of Kiley House and scribbled notes as he skimmed through several books stacked before him: *Walden*, Emerson's *Nature*, Whitman's "Song of Myself." Only his personal cachet had freed the books themselves from the library Rare Books Room. But he couldn't handle audiotapes well enough, hadn't bothered looking for tapes, in fact, and had to have the real article at hand.

By early Sunday evening he was ready.

By midnight Sunday a line had begun to form outside Borgward Hall as those invited made certain of a place inside.

They needn't have worried. Jackie had seen to everything. Within the 400-seat auditorium ropes marked off twenty seats at the front to simulate a classroom. Students had first call on those seats. The remaining 380 places quickly filled with security guards, Faculty, disguised and curious Bizads (Dr. Feenan among them; he looked most like a student), those people lucky enough to have invitations. Invitations were at a premium. Forgeries were more plentiful, just as authentic-appearing, and cheaper-by-barter than the real thing. Dr. Hobart Reid got his by authorizing two oil changes for a black-market cab driver, who got it from Tyrone Floy in prepayment for delivering Tyrone and his friends to the auditorium. Tyrone had made it, copying a real invitation stolen from (?).

Some of these patterns are difficult to untangle.

Kiley walked into the room and wished he hadn't.

No matter how he approached his class, the circus atmosphere in the buzzing, stifling hall would prevent any honest evaluation of the results. He was accustomed to small classes, students hanging on every word (against the likelihood of an exam), and no interference from outsiders.

Not the case today.

He reached the lectern and raised his hands for silence. It drew applause. Another difference from his usual classes. He let the pleasant sound wash over him and tried to narrow his gaze to the rope-enclosed classroom section. All but three of the students there were miniature Kileys, bald, prosthetic-shod, aggressively male.

Still the applause pattered in staccato rhythm.

He waved them quiet. "Please. I know many of you are here for reasons I don't pretend to understand. If you don't mind, I'm going to try ignoring everyone but the class. Is that understood?"

A rumble of assent.

"Fine. And you," he said to the students. Two of them were wrestling in the aisle, another whirled a spool on a string over his head. "You can help most by considering this just one of your normal classes. Is that all right?"

The students who happened to be looking his way nodded. The

rest continued to circulate, climbing over chairbacks and reveling in the spotlight they felt upon them. In a few minutes—which seemed hours, to Kiley's embarrassment—they settled into semi-silence. He recognized Susie Urban in the front row and smiled. It would help to have a friendly face to talk to.

"I'd like to begin by reading something to you, a comment from Thoreau's *Walden*. He—"

"What's 'at?" a boy shouted. He was tiny, miniature, and *not* wearing the costume. His long locks looked out of place among the shaven scalps; his clothes were nondescript, a neutral beige. But something more about him puzzled Kiley. Then he saw it. The boy wore glasses. A quick scan of the packed hall affirmed Kiley's recollection. No one wore glasses any more. He didn't know why. He would have to ask Jackie. On the boy now standing in front of him, the glasses seemed an archaism; he probably had a slide rule in one pocket, too.

"I'm sorry?"

"I say, what's 'at? That *Walden*?"

Kiley smiled. "It's a book, written by a man named Henry David Thoreau. But thank you for the interruption. Any of the rest of you, too. If you have questions, at any time, please feel—"

"Who he?" The same boy again. Kiley decided to name him "Willis."

"Who? Oh. Thoreau? He was a nineteenth-century writer, a naturalist, but I'm sure many of you—"

"You mean he *dead*?" Susie's eyes swelled round, and her jaw hung agape. He could see her tongue.

"Certainly! He lived from 1817 to 1862. Now, if—"

"But good rat, man!" another girl chimed in. "What the fuck we want to know 'bout some dead man for?"

This time the answer didn't come to hand so quickly. Kiley peered at them to see whether it might be an initiation—a test of the new teacher. The bewilderment on their faces seemed honest enough. He couldn't hide a small grin. He raised his eyes from the students to the massed spectators and saw several smiles matching his own.

Well, he could approach his subject as basically as necessary. He laid his notes on the lectern and stepped away to begin pacing. This was more like it, the give and take that he knew and enjoyed.

"Let's start here. I hope in the next few weeks to trace a pattern through American intellectual history. We'll call it 'idealism,' for now, although it differs from the philosophers' more precise use of that term. It was a habit of mind that dominated American thought, American letters, even in some ways American politics, well into the last century. One scholar has written that the Second World War—"

"Mis' Kiley?" Susie Urban raised her hand.

"What!" He took a calming breath and asked again. "I'm sorry. Yes, Miss Urban?" (His words drew a laugh that threw him off balance. Literally. He reached out and seized the lectern to steady himself.) "What is it?"

"Is it somebody here ask you to talk on this 'dealism thing?'" She intended her waving hands to encompass the muttering students. They led Kiley's eyes toward the spectators, where—for the first time—he saw Jackie, sitting quietly a few rows from the front.

Patiently, he explained, "*You* were the one who asked when I would start teaching classes again, weren't you?"

"Uh-huh. Only I want to know, who is it ask you 'bout this 'dealism?"

Wading through the quicksand of her question, he leaned forward; proximity might help her understand. "One of the classes I used to teach was a survey of intellectual trends in American history. The other night I listened to the catalogue of course offerings, and it seems no one else is teaching such a course now. I thought—"

The laughter was more widespread, now from the observers as well as the students. He looked at them in surprise and saw the broad smiles again. This time he understood. They weren't smiling *with* him; they were laughing *at* him. No mistaking the superior smirks written on the gathered faces. Somehow, he was making a fool of himself for their entertainment. But that couldn't be! He knew what he was talking about. Who here knew it better?

With great effort he blanked out the conscious sight of those contemning grins and focused on the notes in his hand. Between his eyes and the notecards swam a disembodied Cheshire rictus.

"Let's get at it this way," he said. He was running out of opening statements. "Many of the suggestions in *The Kiley Proposal* stemmed from—"

"Is it a filum of *Walden* somewheres?" Willis interrupted.

"It's not the sort of book—"

"Or either a tape?" This from one of the spectators. The class was in danger of turning into a free-for-all.

"No. That is, I don't know. Someone may have—"

"Then how we spoze to know 'bout it?"

Susie jumped to her feet, Kiley's champion. "Let him say, dig? Maybe he know somethin we spoze to be doin we ain't. Let him say."

She sat down again and nodded permission for him to continue.

"There's some misunderstanding here. Maybe that's it. If you'll wait till I've finished, I'll be happy to answer questions. Is that all right?"

Before his lips closed he recognized his mistake. By ending with a question, he'd opened Pandora's box. All the students spoke at once, each soprano voice louder, shriller than the others. Through the din, a repeated keening sound marked time, and marked, and finally separated out as a whistle. The students quieted and turned to look at the boy who had started it all. "Willis." He stopped whistling.

"Raht on. 'fore you talk, Ah'm a get somepin straight. We-all's time is full up wif 'portan stuff. But when they ax us to come here and listen to what you puttin down, we say, 'Why not?' It's ever one of us here honor studen's, y'dig? We ain't screw around wif jus any class. But Ah'm assume all the time somebody's let you know what you gon teach. Looks like 'at ain't so. I ain't give a shit what these others do, but if it ain't nobody *ax* you to mess wif this 'dealism jive, why for should I hang around?

"Maybe someday Ah fine out what you know, then *Ah* ax you to teach me it. But sho not 'is stuff, man."

He wrapped himself in dignity and strode up the aisle, in his injured pride standing nearly as tall as the seated spectators.

Later, Kiley would take comfort in the fact that the applause for Willis's oration wasn't unanimous.

When the noise abated, Susie Urban and one black student, Kiley-clad, still sat in the "classroom." The observing audience was intact, their smiles more in evidence and in no way cryptic. Kiley saw thousands of white teeth.

"Mis' Kiley? Why ain't you teach us what you done las weekend?" Susie desperately sought a neutral subject that might suit his competence.

He couldn't think of an answer. His roving eye found Jackie, who was nodding helpfully. He cleared his throat.

He made three false starts before giving up.

No inspiration. Nothing.

32

HUMBLED, Kiley took his wounded ego into Jackie's comforting arms. There was no need for false humility. His was real, and massive enough to choke an air duct. Defeat was all it took to patch his quarrel with Jackie, as though the madness of that morning had proven him wrong and her—by contrast—right. Or, so Jackie understood it. Kiley understood nothing. He let the tide take him.

Even after she had whispered in his burning ear a list of his *faux pas*, he was less than comforted. How could he know, for example, that "Urban" was a synonym for "bastard"? Publicly calling Susie by her last name had made him seem a tactless nitwit, but—after all—she had used it first, that night in the Fac lounge.

"'at don't signify," Jackie said. "She got to say it. But it ain't right to insult her like that with her friends around."

"She didn't look insulted. She was the only one polite enough to—"

"Looks is one thing. Likely she have a crush on you, 'sall. Kids is like that. Now, I don't want to say I told you so, only you did go chargin in there without askin me for tip one. I'm sorry it come out like it done. But it ain't for good and all. Probably there's lots of things you can teach. Onliest thing is, we gon have to find out what."

Her comforting didn't really help. He found his own consolation. In the wreckage of his teaching aspirations lay a decision, ready-made for him. It would be a cold and rainy day inside the university forcefield before he faced a class again. His pride couldn't stand another such beating.

As if to help him further, a call from Bengston eliminated one more possibility from his future.

"Bob-oh?" Bengston's shaggy eyebrows danced a question on the vidphone screen. "Have you had enough? I wasn't there this morning, but Feenan—uh, one of my people was. He tells me you probably see now why it's so important that our program gets adopted."

"How does that follow? I'll admit things didn't go as well as I'd hoped, but why assume I'm suddenly in your corner? Would it have been any different with your students out there?"

"Absolutely. There you've done it again. Hit right to the truth of the matter. It's one of the things I like about you, Bob. Now, firstly, we never let our students collect in such big numbers. And secondly, no instructor actually faces them when they're in circuit with the teaching equipment. If you'll recall our little demonstration the other day, fourthly, I feel you'll see my point. No smart mouth from any of *our* students. A touch of current and they're meek as mice. That foolishness today comes from treating them like adults. I feel—"

"Adults? I didn't see many of them, either. I got overmatched with a pack of spoiled teeny-boppers. Sorry. You don't know the term," he answered Bengston's puzzled look. "But if I have to choose sides in this madhouse, it damn sure won't be with someone whose idea of fun is wiring little kids."

Bengston's expression spelled pompous. He puffed his cheeks like a nesting hamster, his head swayed back on his ramrod spine. "I'm disappointed that you take that attitude, Robert. It's clear to me that you can't identify whom your real friends are. Think of this. If it hadn't of been for all my efforts, you might still be locked away in that storage drawer. Don't you feel you owe me—"

"Was that a *favor?* Get stuffed!" He broke the connection.

Jackie's hand slipped into his. He let himself be led into the bedroom, where she pointed at a bottled water dispenser. His eyes showed a resignation he didn't have to express; one more mystery, to him.

She whispered an explanation and promised better days to come.

33

"[One] got started with it [COPE ("Committee on Premium Education")] and might as well see it through. [I] feel like a juggler in a high wind."

The Notebooks of Robert Kiley
(as edited)

IN THE MORNING, Kiley made a decision. When no thunderclap followed, he was disappointed. He and Jackie had discussed his dilemma for several midnight hours. Each time they had returned to a single solution. He had to make a choice, there was no other way. He lacked her confidence that simply announcing his choice would clear away all the tangling arguments that held him trapped; but she said it would work. And she knew the enemy better than he did.

They made his decision. After two brief phone calls to arrange matters for him, Jackie led the way down the rickety staircase to the street. No cab, this time. A car stood waiting—a black limousine bearing the initials UN (Urban *News*) emblazoned on the door panel, beneath the picture of a newshawk and his camera.

Jackie held the car door open and spoke to a figure half hidden inside. "Doctor Rudnick. This here Mis' Kiley."

"Opensky to see you, sir. And awfully pleased to be of some assistance." Rudnick made a circle of his thumb and forefinger, then snapped himself in the crotch.

Kiley winced. For several reasons.

A chauffeur guided the silent car away from the curb.

On their way to the trivee station Rudnick showered them with a steady gush of hip inanity. His comments were a tangle of muddled slang and self-aggrandizement. He recited the entire day's broadcast schedule in response to no request at all, described every piece of equipment involved in the actual transmission process, commented on sights visible through the car's polarized windows, and generally tried to entertain.

After one glance at Rudnick's cosmetic beauty, Kiley tuned him out and concentrated instead on the speech he and Jackie had decided he would have to make. Nothing flowery, no special rhetoric, merely an announcement of his intention to join the Fac cause. That would serve notice on all and sundry that he was no longer on the open market; and it would define him—to himself, as well as to all the viewers. Summarized: he would tell them that he was the Robert Kiley of *The Kiley Proposal*. (No one seemed inclined to let him think otherwise.) Like Noah's saying, "Looks like rain."

The choice had really been easy to make, the path of least resistance. If he had to align himself with one of the power blocs, Fac was the obvious one. Certainly not the students, who had only anger on their side; nor Bizads, with their pompous neo-behaviorism. His options had faded. It was now go with Fac or give up any claim to power. He was certainly not that foolish. There is a reassuring ring to the phrase *carte blanche*.

". . . wonderful staff," Rudnick babbled. "All just delightfully involved in our labors for the common good and willing to simply work their ass off." His voice rumbled in theatrical resonance, Arthur Godfrey in an echo chamber. "Many of us, you recognize, might have made it on the national nets, but rat that. We have a duty to the public. With us gone, who would inform them? Ahhh, but sometimes. . . ." His eyes glistened as he manfully refrained from describing his sacrifice. One manicured hand brushed at the mass of silver curls spilling boyishly over his tanned forehead.

Jackie commiserated with Rudnick's plight. Kiley listened.

By the time they pulled into a garage a few blocks from Kiley House, Dr. Rudnick had made his point. His was a talent wasted here at Urban U. Many of his friends thought he might have had a career in films—he waved a modest hand at the suggestion—but he admitted to a streak of the missionary in himself. Jackie said she understood.

She really did.

Kiley understood too, but didn't care. He felt like a battery in need of recharging. He wasn't ready to take on the salvation of J. Cameron Rudnick, not with his own power waning so badly.

Several bustling technicians and staff announcers gathered around and led the trio down a long corridor. None of them penetrated Kiley's preoccupation. When they left him at a large, leather-covered door, he remembered only hundreds of capped teeth. He was surrounded by carnivores.

Rudnick ushered them inside the studio and took command. "Set?"

Nods from two men on the floor, one behind a camera. And a filtered voice from the glassed-in control booth rasped, "Ready when you are, Jay Cee." Strained laughter.

"Stand on the light mark and say whatever you like. If you get nervous—we know you're not a professional," Rudnick forgave Kiley's probable inadequacy. "If you get windy, rat it. We can edit or retake. We'll cast it every break today and tonight."

Kiley walked stiff-legged to a dot of light glowing faintly on the tiled floor. He faced the camera. One of the floor managers pointed a finger at him. He heard himself recite, "Good morn— Uh, hello. I'm Robert Kiley. I wanted—"

The floor manager glanced at Rudnick, ran a hand over his scalp, and pantomimed, "Who else?" Kiley paused in confusion.

He began again, urged on by Rudnick's violent nodding and Jackie's confident smile. "I'm Robert Kiley. I wanted to take this opportunity to thank all of you who've been so kind to me the past few days. Uh, weeks. I would also like to mention that, although I can never repay your kindness, I have agreed to represent the university at the next federal budget hearings. If you have any particular requests that haven't been heard, please get in touch with Doctor Peter Clausewitz in the Department of Humanities. He and I will be working closely together on the budget proposals."

He stopped in relief, then felt egg on his face: The camera still threatened him with a red light; Rudnick wore a peeved frown.

"Oh. And I would like to thank Doctor Rudnick for giving me this chance to speak with you."

The light went dead. Rudnick's face came to life. And the floor managers rushed to congratulate him. "Hey, great, Mister Kiley!" "Sure you never done this before?" "Just like a pro."

He hardly felt them pounding his back as he walked from the studio, through a knot of cheering admirers, down the corridor, and into a lounge.

Still no thunderclap.

With Rudnick and Jackie, he sat at a conference table and dawdled away twenty minutes over a cup of coffee, one eye on a monitor and clock mounted on the far wall. A sweep second hand marked the half hour. . . .

FANFARE.

DEPTH-TAKE HOLOGRAM MONTAGE, fading through:

> KILEY ON OPERATING TABLE
> KILEY WITH PREXY HALLER
> MISC. CLIPS KILEY ON STREET
> KILEY BEFORE CLASS

Voice over
Urban University Networks, under
the direction of Doctor J. Cameron
Rudnick, present Mister Robert
Kiley

DIRECT CUT:
CLOSE ON KILEY, fade FANFARE to muted VIOLINS, b.g.

Kiley
I'm Robert Kiley. (HARP GLIS-
SANDO, fading) I want to take
this opportunity to thank all of you

ZOOM OUT, MEDIUM ON KILEY, SUPERED ON CROWD
SCENE, crowd cheering silently

Kiley (cont.)
who've been so kind to me the past
few

GO THROUGH SUPER TO SUPERED CALENDAR, pages flipping

Kiley (cont.)
days. Uh, weeks. Although I can
never repay your kindness,

DIRECT CUT:
CLOSE ON KILEY, TILT UP, backlight for halo effect

Kiley (cont.)
I have agreed to represent the university (add muted FANFARE,
b.g.) at the next federal

GO THROUGH BACKLIGHT TO STOCK SHOT, CAPITOL

Kiley (cont.)
budget hearings. If you have any
particular requests that haven't
been heard, please get in touch
with Doctor

SPLITSCREEN, quarter inset lower right CLAUSEWITZ, KILEY, upper left three-quarters, ECU

> Kiley (cont.)
> Peter Clausewitz in the Department of Humanities.

SLOW FADE CLAUSEWITZ, FULLSCREEN ECU KILEY

> Kiley (cont.)
> He and I will be working closely together on the budget proposals. And I would like to thank

DIRECT CUT:

ECU RUDNICK

> Kiley (cont., o.s.)
> Doctor (MIMIC INSERT: "J. Cameron") Rudnick for giving me this chance to speak with you. (build FANFARE)

SLOW DISSOLVE:

STATION ID CARD

It was nearly a thunderclap. Impressive.

"How did you do that so fast?" Kiley asked.

"Creative editing," Rudnick shrugged in humility. "We couldn't treat you otherwise, Mister Kiley."

"It *did* go pretty well, didn't it?"

They nodded.

"Makings of a real performer there," Rudnick said. "I can spot it every time, that spark, that charisma. If you ever think about a new career, Mister Kiley, come and talk to me about it. I'd be happy to advise you myself, personally. Get you over some of your clumsiness. You know, I can—"

"Thanks." His moment spoiled, Kiley walked out.

Jackie caught him in the corridor. "It's a car waiting outside to take us back, 'less you wants to go somewhere else."

"Back is fine."

They walked out into the green haze, Rudnick watching from the doorway. They were only twenty feet from the waiting car when a rifle bullet caught Kiley high in the shoulder and slammed him to the ground.

34

"While the Committee of course abhors violence, we would point not to the specific acts of student unrest but to the underlying causes of those acts. The good doctor treats neither the symptoms of a disease nor the disease itself, but the patient. We are concerned with the patient."

The Kiley Proposal

TIME DID strange things. Within an imaginary sphere surrounding Kiley, it slowed. Outside that sphere it accelerated.

He felt a fiery claw pluck at his shoulder. His right shoulder. In resignation, he thought, *Again! Why does everything happen to me twice?* A gout of blood spurted down the sleeve of his new coat. He watched with irritation while he fell in a lazy, twisting spiral toward the ground that seemed to rise cautiously, slowly toward him. The ground hit him on his left side. It fell away again to leave him hovering and settling gently like a wafted leaf. The artificial turf caught and cradled him. A part of his mind counted two bounces when he hit. His knees crept toward his face in a misting haze. Then there was a forest of legs surrounding him. It all took hours.

At the same time a melee of shouting figures burst into a mad hora. Jackie choked back a scream with knotted fists, and four security guards materialized from the very ground to circle Kiley's falling form. They lunged toward one another like the sides of a box imploding on its contents, while a honking siren blatted pain through the din of yelling voices, unintelligible commands; and there was a general sense of running. Motion was the rule.

Jackie's face appeared among the gathered legs. She began to jerk at his jacket. Each tug tore his arm from its socket. He rolled to escape her aid. One of the security men stepped on his hand. Cars came and went. A short, greasy man in a torn bathrobe knocked Jackie aside and shouted curses at anyone within earshot. A man in white dropped a half-filled balloon over Kiley's face.

It grew dark and peaceful where Kiley was.

On the other side of the balloon it was still hectic. The man in white used a small air gun with joyful abandon. Each time he pointed it someone fell smiling to the ground. Soon only the doctor in white, Morgan in his torn bathrobe, and Morgan's personal security guards stood erect.

They carried Kiley to a waiting car and left everyone else smiling on the ground.

Dr. J. Cameron Rudnick, who had been watching through the open door, sent a newshawk out to revive and interview the bodies.

35

"These months wasted on this [deleted] proposal and [I] still don't know who's got the real power."

> *The Notebooks of Robert Kiley*
> (as edited)

KILEY AND MORGAN had a long conversation. Some would call it a verbal fencing match. Each tried to test the other's defenses, to discover what response an emergency might evoke. Kiley learned more, perhaps because he had already experienced Morgan's efficiency. No analogue existed to feed Morgan's curiosity: Kiley's actions to this point have been mundane and notable more in their lack of efficacy than in their distinctiveness.

"You've had a watch on me the whole time?" Kiley asked. He lay on a couch in Morgan's office and gingerly touched his already-healing shoulder.

Morgan paced.

"Might put it that way. But don't think of it as spying. Where would you be now if I hadn't kept track of you?"

"Your point. I'm just not happy with the idea. It makes me feel like a goldfish."

"You are. Everyone's keeping an eye on you. Be surprised at how many tails I've had to pull off your back. Bizads trailing you, Faculty, those nut kids, everybody. But you weren't in any danger, not till that fool announcement this morning." He peered at Kiley to gauge his reaction.

"It seemed like the best idea. What I don't understand is why someone took a shot at—"

"Jesus, man! You were begging for it. You attract trouble." Morgan snatched a pear from a basket of fruit on his desk and lectured through the juice dribbling down his chin. "Minute you opened your mouth you set all sorts of gears grinding. My people called me on it, and I sent the guard out. Can bet others were just as fast. No more than three or four minutes between the announcement and that kid's shot. How fast do you—?"

"Then you know who it was?" Kiley felt something like relief surging through him. A defined enemy is easier to avoid.

"Well, no. Not certain. But think about it. It's not Bengston's style. He'll do anything short of murder to get what he wants, but he *will* stop at that. At least, I think he will.

"So that leaves the kids who hauled you off to the air ducts the other day. Some of them are hyped up half the time. Retardo and meth can give you a pretty stiff high, and they're so caught up in their revolutionary games they're liable to try anything. They're the likely candidates."

"If you know where they are, why don't you do something about them?"

"None of my business. Internal affairs belong to you locals. Long as the ledgers balance and Haller doesn't do some damn fool thing like passing out real currency, whatever else happens here is out of my hands."

"It must be nice. None of this matters to you, is that it?"

"Some ways it does. Want a pear?" Morgan wiped his hands on his trouser legs and picked up the basket of fruit to offer it. "No? Okay. But help yourself."

He disappeared behind his desk to rummage through a drawer, then stood waving a sheaf of papers. "Here's the budget I've been working out for next year. All accounted for. If you're going to Washington with me, I ought to fill you in on a few things. Here, for instance." He flipped through the papers looking for something as he walked toward the couch.

"Here's. . . . You *can* read, isn't that right?"

Kiley nodded and found himself surprised at his reaction. Only weeks—weeks, plus some fifty years—only weeks earlier the question would have seemed an insult. Now it was part of a context he accepted.

"Okay then. Here's where the Fac budget starts. Flip through it till you see something you don't understand. Just ask. I'll try and explain things."

He dumped the bundle of forms in Kiley's lap and ducked back behind his huge desk.

After a moment of incomprehension, Kiley heard humming. Out of the corner of his eye he caught sight of Morgan's smugness. Then he couldn't admit his ignorance.

"It looks all right. Clausewitz described it to me."

"Maybe. But don't go too much by that guy. He doesn't know his hat from his ass."

Kiley passed the test. His face immobile, he walked over to return the papers.

"Fine," Morgan said. "I think we can work together. And glad you decided to make the trip."

"It's not all that final," Kiley said. "It's still up to President Haller, so far as—"

"Skip Haller. He's happy stretched out in front of the trivee. If I say you're going with me, it's settled."

Kiley kneaded his shoulder. The pain was gone, only a slight stiffness remained.

"Still bother you? It shouldn't. I had the doc—"

"It's okay." Kiley hunted for an innocuous way of putting his next question. "I get the feeling you want me along with you. Rather than someone else, I mean."

Morgan shrugged. "Doesn't matter that much. There are some people who'd like to meet you, and you might enjoy the trip, but I can't force you to go. Entirely up to you," Morgan lied.

Kiley heard the intensity behind the false unconcern. He did want to go. What did Morgan's reasons matter? It came to the same thing in any case. "It's a deal, then. When do we leave?"

Morgan snatched up another pear and bit into it to cover his broad smile. "Two weeks," he mumbled. "Why don't you and I get together tomorrow? Talk about a few things you ought to know before we take on Congress."

"One thing, though."

Morgan paused warily, eyebrows raised, his chewing jaw halted.

"Doctor Muller goes with us."

"Hmmmm. Well, let me explain something. The law says—"

"She goes, or I don't."

Morgan's grin looked painful. "Certainly. I can see that. We'll work out something. But let's talk—"

"There's nothing to 'work out.'"

A strip of pear skin fluttered between Morgan's front teeth. He scraped it free with a dirty thumbnail and licked it off. "I said all right, didn't I?" His eyes weren't smiling.

Kiley's were.

"Power" is the operative word.

"And one other thing. I want a bodyguard from now till we leave. I can't depend on your security types. They were damn near too late this morning."

"Already taken care of that." Morgan bent over and shouted into his desk. "Wallace?"

The outer door opened and a small man entered. He looked to be nearing fifty, mousey, unobtrusive, subservient.

"Him?"

"That's exactly why, 'him.' Nobody ever sees Wallace." Morgan turned to the man. "Blend with the wallpaper, don't you, Wallace?"

"Yes sir."

"Think you can take care of our friend here?"

Wallace nodded. No demonstration of judo, no weapons display—simply a touch of confidence about him. For no reason Kiley could name, it was convincing.

"Now, you go with Wallace. We've got you a new place to stay, for the next few days, at least. A rat couldn't get in. If anyone tries we'll *know* who's gunning for you."

"Where are we—"

"You'll see. Doctor Muller's already there, waiting. Now. Let me get back to work. Unless you have any questions."

Kiley followed Wallace out. At the door Kiley glanced back to see Morgan wiping a wet smear off the budget forms with his shirtsleeve.

36

"Programs being canceled [owing to lack of funds] and the Dean's office [has recently been] redecorated. [One sees] special privileges all over the place."

The Notebooks of Robert Kiley
(as edited)

JACKIE WAS WAITING for him in the Presidential Suite of the University Hotel. It might seem strange for a closed community to contain a hotel; after all, everyone in the university has a home. Everyone but the students in the counter-U and other criminals who have had their purchase cards destroyed. But even here, the habit of vacations remains. Members of the university are not so different from other people. Many of them marry and need a honeymoon retreat. Those inclined to test their worth to the community occasionally spend a day or two at the University Hotel, if only to find out whether their purchase cards will be accepted. On any day in the year scores of guests wander the hotel corridors, dance in the Ballroom, occupy themselves in the Gameroom. It is a popular place. It stands on Skinner Avenue, across from University Park.

When Kiley entered the Presidential Suite, Jackie was waiting for him.

He calmed her fears, explained the interview with Morgan—she was impressed—and told her about Wallace. Better to get their quarrel over now, if the fact of a bodyguard would set her temper off again.

She opened the door and peered out at Wallace, who stood beside a plastic rubber plant in the corridor, blending with the decor as instructed. The sight reassured her; her presence was still necessary to Kiley's well-being. A nondescript cipher like Wallace was no threat to her self-defined position.

"Don't look like much, does he," she said with some pleasure.

Kiley agreed and toured the suite.

Three rooms—bedroom, sitting room, kitchen, all furnished in classic Swedish Modern—and a bath. Not a sonic booth, a real shower.

Childlike in her delight, Jackie reached past him to turn on the shower. "See. Water! And no limits. When Morgan do for you, he know how to fix things up. It ain't no better suite in the whole university. Now you know how Morgan feel."

"Maybe. For his own reasons. We'll see."

"Awwww! You gettin worse'n 'at ole Sister Chiu, always lookin for somethin suspicious. Enjoy it. It's Christmas in a couple days. You know a better place to spend it?"

He let himself be led to the glass wall overlooking University Park, pleased without understanding the excitement Jackie displayed.

"Here now. You just watch." She pointed across the street toward the park.

"What am I supposed—"

"Be patient. I hear it on the news not a minute ago. Look at all them peoples gatherin 'round."

She was right. On Skinner Avenue below, a crowd had begun to congregate, some walking into the park itself, others milling in the street. Many of them seemed bald ice-skaters, skimming along in their cumbersome Kiley shoes: students. His fans.

"There! Now look!" She pointed up.

A vortex was forming in the forcefield shell overhead. Crackling light marked a whirlpool of green that swirled and circled, then faded away. And the field dilated open. Rain entered.

To Jackie, eyes sparkling in wonder, it was actually raining.

To Kiley, it was only raining.

"Is this the excitement?"

"Isn't it? They said on the news, rain outside, and they has to water the park. You ever see anything like that?"

He wanted to say "yes," but he felt protective. He saw no reason to spoil her fun. He found a way to enjoy it all himself. The crowd below had divided into two groups—the curious, who stood and watched; the adventuresome, who dashed past the cordon of security guards into the park itself and gamboled in the falling rain.

"Here. Lemme show you better," Jackie said. She flipped a switch beneath the window.

Kiley jumped back as water sprayed over the outside of the glass, then scores of small wipers dropped from their overhead channel and cleaned away the filthy particles obscuring the view. In a moment he could see perfectly. One green spot in the middle of the university, the park below, with all the little people dashing about in the cold drizzle.

And he standing high above it.

No sight had pleased him more since his arrival.

He standing above it.

"What's it called again?" he asked.

"University Park, 'sall. Why?"

"Nothing. Just thinking. The way they change names around here, it wouldn't surprise me if someone got the bright idea to call it 'Kiley Park' one of these days.

"Not that I'd allow that, you understand. Just thinking."

37

TYRONE FLOY, Kiley-clad for disguise, shivered in the cold drizzle. He stood huddled beneath the sparse, bare branches of a dying ash tree and watched his troops dashing back and forth over the park grass. More than the cold made him tremble: like so many of the children testing themselves at the moment, he was frightened by the very notion of being under an open sky. Forcefield, to him, was nature's way. Even to think of anything else made him edgy.

Tricia Neely stood beside him; but she stood straight, as tall as possible, determined not to show how little she enjoyed the rain that made Tyrone so obviously uncomfortable. Months without Retardo prevented her stripping to the waist as Tyrone had. She wore a gray coverall.

"Okay. I'm here. What's doing?" Tyrone demanded.

"See the window up there, the high one? That's where he is now." Tricia pointed toward the top of the hotel.

"So? Didn't you get your rocks off good enough this ame? You know I told you not to try that shooting stuff. Now you drag me out in the open to peek at a window. If he's in there, he's out of reach."

"Maybe. Maybe no. They didn't get me this ame, they won't pay attention now, not with all this excitement." She sneered at the children playing fearfully in the unaccustomed shower and stood posed in superiority. "You had your chance to come with us. We almost got him, too. Didn't I tell you why he was going to the trivee shop?"

"You told me. And I told *you*. No killing. Not till I give the word. I don't care if you start giving me mouth when we're lone-

some this way. When we're in family, out it. All you do is confuse
the others. One leader's opensky. Too many makes garbage."

She leaned close and rubbed a warm hand over his chest. "Come
down, Tyrone. You still think I'm calling you? I just want to let you
know what I see. You're leader, no argument. Only when do we
move on him? You said it yourself—long as he's out front, nobody
listens to us."

He smiled down at her. "There's ways. I'll let you know."

Her groping hand found thin curls on his chest. She tangled
her fingers in the hair, and jerked. "When?" Then jumped away.

"You little sky-sucker! What the rat you doing? That hurt!" He
rubbed his chest, massaging away the pain, yet pleased at her attention. "You expect me to go charging into the hotel and start twisting his arm in front of Wallace? He'd eat me alive, and you know
it."

She danced around, taunting him. "Afraid, Tyrone? What you
scared of, Wallace or me? Huh? Let's *do* something! We're no closer
to opensky than we were months ago. And you said Kiley was the
key, ain't so? Where's your key now? Up there, living fat. You think
the others will hang around waiting for you to get your Kiley on?"

He blushed in the darkness and made a swipe at her with one
hand. He missed, and she danced farther away.

"I mean it, Tyrone. I'm waiting for a man. When do you think
you'll make it. Hey, Tyrone? Hey? When do you think?"

He lunged after her, caught her by one arm, and spun her to the
wet grass, knocking the breath from both of them.

They lay gasping for a moment.

"You okay?" he asked.

"Hummm? You want to squeeze me some, *Mister* Tyrone?
What do you think the man's doing up there in his tower?" She drew
his head onto her chest and kneaded the top of his head with her
chin. "Maybe you're my man, after all, *Mister* Tyrone. I'm getting
hints, you know?"

Laughing, he pushed her away. "I'll give you more than hints.
Only not now. Not here. Tricia, you're the damndest alley cat I ever

saw. Half the time I don't know what you're after. If sex is it, maybe you got the wrong guy. There's more blowing than that. You think Kiley's sexing now, right? So what? Am I Kiley? I got something else in my head you're going to like."

She lifted his face and fixed him with her blazing eyes. "Do it! Now, man. Do it! Nobody'll even blink. We walk right in like we belong there. Right up the elevator. You said it, who sees a nigger? We'll be in his room before—"

"Rat that garbage." Awkwardly, he scrambled to his knees. "I'm telling it. Get the others and bring them along. Down to Twenty-duct, not home. We're not touching the man tonight. We're going outside!"

He swelled proudly in the glow of her amazement. She clambered to her feet in slow motion as if she were glass and might shatter any moment.

"Outside?"

"While you were off this peem, I did some figuring. I got a way out. Tonight."

"But Tyrone. What if—"

"Move it!" He slapped her bottom. "Twenty-duct. One hour. I'll show you the way. Not to worry, Tricia. We're going outside. Get the others."

He watched her walk away uncertainly, watched till she had spoken to three of the children exhausted from their games and lying face down in the rain. Then he tensed his thumb and forefinger and snapped a derisive greeting at the lighted window high atop the University Hotel.

38

FIVE SEALED train cars clanked up the long incline toward Exit East. Inside the control room, Ethel Pease slipped one hand into a waldo, flexed her fingers, and watched the extensor counterpart outside mimic her actions. She reached for the exit authorization tape cartridge clipped to the first car and jerked it loose. A small movement of her wrist drew the cartridge toward her control booth. She dropped it into the receptor slot. Chuckling, grating sounds clattered in her ear as relays closed, data slipped through the read-out sensors and appeared on the screen beside her: car destination, volume, weight, content density (for the X-ray check), special instructions—all of it appeared as numbers and accompanying colored lights on the screen.

She released the waldo and turned to the bank of dials beneath the screen itself. By trial and error she managed to match numbers and colors on the top row—the tape-dictated row—to numbers and colors that she imprinted on the bottom row. When all the colors and numbers matched, she pressed the release button.

The cars inched toward the exit gate. Each was subjected to a series of tests to determine whether the contents of the car—weight, volume, and so on—matched the exit tapes. It was all automatic. It always worked.

A synapse closed in Ethel Pease's brain. She began to recite her colors. It was almost automatic. But the touch of creativity present in what might be called the "personality" of Ethel Pease allowed for leeway. Some nights she ran through her colors from black to white, some nights infrared to ultraviolet. Tonight was different. It would take some time for all five exiting cars to be processed through the automatic equipment. Another synapse closed, and Ethel Pease evaluated the time remaining to her as she sat before the read-out screen. "Long time," something told her.

She smiled. Now she could show off, if only for her own satisfaction. Though her job didn't require such knowledge, Ethel Pease knew all of the 267 Munsell color chips. She began to recite them: hue, lightness, saturation, chromatics—across the ranks and down the files.

She had reached strong purple/purple when the emergency siren began to whine.

It triggered a reaction in Ethel Pease. She acted instinctively in the sequence intended to trap escapees: her left hand closed the exit port, right hand flipped a switch to summon security guards, left knee depressed a stud that lit the interior of the exit chamber, right hand brushed over the FLOOD control, left hand pushed her away from the console, and she whirled toward the ladder leading to the overhead catwalk. "CHECK MASTER CONTROLS" blared silently in her mind.

Lunging toward the ladder, she failed to see the off-load door on the first car swing open.

Curled in on himself like a fetus inside the huge casting, Tyrone Floy flinched when the siren erupted. He shouted a warning and grabbed Tricia's hand to drag her from the casting beside him and leap for the door.

Before they hit the floor the water had risen two feet. They splashed shouting through the flood, three other children right behind them, and clambered over the rear retaining wall.

They dashed breathless back down the long incline toward the nearest air duct, scrambled off the tracks and into the intake duct so quickly that the approaching security guards got off only three shots. One of the children lay dead at the duct mouth, a gaping crater of singed meat smoldering in his punctured side; but Tyrone and the others were safe.

The security guards burst into the Exit East control booth. All clear. Nothing amiss.

Ethel Pease stood atop the catwalk with her hands clutching one of the huge rheostat wheels. Green, green, yellow, yellow, gray, gray.

39

CHRISTMAS WILL FALL on a Wednesday that year. Students in the Department of Christianity (pictograph: crimson cross on white background) will celebrate the holiday in a traditional way. Many departments will suspend classes. Out of deference. A few of the conservative professors in the Department of Folklore (pictograph: green troll under a bridge being crossed by three white goats) will behead a virgin chicken raised especially for that rite. But in the main, Christmas will be a time of gift-receiving and celebration of midwinter recess.

It will be at times like this that Kiley remembers his own boyhood. In rural Illinois where he grew up—so far as he may be said to have grown up—there were evergreens decorated in every house. His mother had made mincemeat pies, oyster stew on Christmas Eve, sugar cookies in the shape of Santa Claus: Christmas in the Kiley household had been a time of eating and relaxing.

Two days before Christmas, 2024, Robert Kiley will go shopping.

He and Wallace took an armored electric limousine and drove to the Department of Faculty Apparel, where he bought Jackie an umbrella. The spines were rusted, it wouldn't open properly, but then she had no use for it in the university anyway. He thought it would please her, not for a wall-hung display, as the salesman assured him it was intended, but to carry on their forthcoming trip to Washington.

Wallace stayed within two paces of him all the time, furtive eyes glancing in all directions, watchful yet unobtrusive. Like a mongoose.

Back in the armored car Kiley asked to be driven through the park.

"Vehicles not allowed, Mister Kiley," the chauffeur said through the intercom.

Kiley looked at Wallace.

"Do it," Wallace said.

The chauffeur turned the car. It bumped up over the curb and began to score tire tracks in the sod. They circled and crossed the park several times until Kiley snapped, "Here! Stop here."

Kiley borrowed Wallace's laser, climbed from the car, and cut down a small fir tree. He loaded it, trunk still smoldering, in the front seat with the chauffeur and was driven back across Skinner Avenue to the hotel entrance.

"A Christmas tree," he shouted to Jackie, standing in the open doorway. "Now all we need is some ornaments."

Speechless, she looked past Kiley at Wallace.

Wallace raised both hands and shook his head.

Jackie swallowed whatever she had planned to say and listened to Kiley's excited babbling as he organized their Christmas celebration.

Nothing in the next two days was allowed to interfere. He refused to talk to Clausewitz. Morgan had assured him that the budget was all set, that Clausewitz could add to it nothing but confusion in any case. There was also a call from Howard Bengston, a desperate sort of eleventh-hour appeal; Kiley stayed out of sight and let Jackie answer for him. He enjoyed Bengston's vehemence and determination but wouldn't talk to him. Morgan had everything arranged. There was no need to involve anyone else in their plans. Besides, he was interested in Christmas, and in the honeymoon his stay in the hotel had become.

The hotel has its own, untreated water supply.

For Christmas Eve Kiley arranged a surprise. At eleven-thirty, as he and Jackie sat watching trivee, Wallace knocked on their door. Kiley lifted his arm from her shoulders and pantomimed surprise, though it was all he could do to conceal his anticipation.

She pleaded for a hint. He merely shook his head. They followed Wallace through the empty corridor to the Ballroom, strains of an archaic Mantovani waltz inviting them in.

Jackie stopped suddenly. "But . . . where is everyone? It's empty."

"Merry Christmas," Kiley said. "It's for you."

"This?" She stared at the decorated ballroom, the orchestra, a table set for two across the huge empty floor. "But where's everyone else?"

"Just us. Our private party." He strode on ahead and led her to the table.

Wallace closed the double doors and stationed himself outside. The orchestra began to play again.

For an hour they sat enjoying a meal especially prepared for Jackie: oyster stew, mincemeat pie, sugar cookies in the shape of Santa Claus. And they danced, in spite of Kiley's clumsiness.

They danced till nearly three.

Then they could no longer maintain the charade of gaiety; the empty room became depressing. Neither of them was able to look at the orchestra members; they felt too much in the spotlight.

They left. Kiley nodded to Wallace as they passed him in the hall. When they reached the door of their suite they looked back to see people in evening dress filing into the empty ballroom.

Jackie posed a silent question with her eyes.

"Lots of time left for them. It's Christmas for another"—he checked his watch—"for another twenty-one hours. We couldn't go in there with a mob like that, could we? So I fixed it. Merry Christmas."

"Thank you."

When Kiley came out of the shower, Jackie had already taken something for her headache and fallen asleep.

40

HOLIDAYS MEAN different things to different people.

For three days preceding Christmas, university water systems are merely chlorinated. No antirect at all. For most nonstudents holidays mean a return to ardor, though few understand why that is true.

We have seen Kiley's holiday begin. There are other versions of Christmas under way at the same time. More precisely, within the university there are 153 versions of Christmas being celebrated, many thousand versions of Xmas, 356 Hanukkahs, 33 Ramadans, 16 Black Masses, and so on. Homes and apartments are decorated with plastic shrubbery of all varieties—toyon, crab cactus, dagger fern, hellebore or Christmas rose, bushes, branches, holly berries, leaves, pine cones, juniper berries, China berries, currant, quince, cumquat, raisin, and mistletoe. In only one hotel suite is there a real, once-living, Christmas tree. Its presence there marks Kiley as special, a judgment no one could deny.

Few persons in the university, fewer than Kiley assumes, give Robert Kiley even a fleeting thought on this day of celebration.

Tyrone Floy endures a family gathering. With his father and mother he watches the traditional triveecast of *Rudolph the Red-Nosed Reindeer* and secretly fumes at the budding rebellion within the ranks of his fellow conspirators: Tricia Neely has called him out, challenged his authority before the entire group. That night he hears his parents in sex, a holiday ritual as fixed as the special menus allowed. Their murmurs offer a clue, complete a pattern of inference Tyrone had begun to formulate. He vows to eat and drink only sealed, packaged (stolen) specialty foods, every day in the year.

Ethel Pease spends her Christmas in the parents' bleachers at the Department of Child Care, through a one-way window watching and waiting to see Warren open his present.

Peter Clausewitz shares his Christmas with three of his students. All are shorter than he.

Hobart Reid puts final touches on a scholarly tape intended once and for all to refute the popular notion of reindeer as a viable motive force for cross-country transportation.

Ling Chiu, for the fifth consecutive year, recites the stewartalk "Night Before Christmas" into her notetaker and plays it back repeatedly. Her inflection, enunciation, stress patterns, pitch, attack —all remain pure; and yet the recording troubles her. She knows that Stewart overlooked something. If she can define that "something," Lingo may yet replace stewartalk.

J. Cameron Rudnick stars in a triveecast of *The Gift of the Magi*, playing all parts, producing, directing, and dubbing in applause. When he receives the watchfob from himself, and gives himself the ornate combs for his (false) hair, he cries (real) tears.

Howard Bengston devotes his day to curing his wife's stammer, and incidentally testing a miniaturized home-training machine that works on simple 110 current. By evening Ms. Bengston stammers only when she tries to speak. She does not try often.

Morgan eats an entire watermelon and counts the days until he may leave the university.

Jackie Muller has no Christmas of her own, but is allowed to share in Robert Kiley's Christmas.

President Haller doesn't know that December 25 is Christmas.

And we? We will not be in a university in 2024. We will be somewhere in Middle America, under a crisp, clear sky, cracking walnuts and lying to our grandchildren. Or great-grandchildren.

41

THE INTERIOR of Morgan's railway car is splendid. Certain words get overworked, chewed, and mangled till they lose their honest value. Everyone has heard of scores of great inventors, this great president, that great athlete. "Great," in those contexts, comes to mean "above average," if it means anything at all. Consider "splendid," applied with all serious intent to sunsets and face soap, overshoes and underwear. In our present usage, none of those implied nonmeanings will obtain. Morgan's railway car is really splendid.

It is a hurtling shell of coruscating light.

Below waist level, the car is lined with hand-rubbed paneling, limed oak and bird's-eye maple, pine and poplar, each knot and worm gall polished till the very walls will seem to wink. The carpet glistens, too. Not gaudy fur or plasticene, it's simple nylon pile, nylon interlaced with glossy copper cilia. Whispered music wafting from those miniature antennae hovers just below the verge of conscious recognition: Morgan rides amid the implications of a symphony. Each winking quarter panel of the wall bears on it inlaid ebony in pictographs designed to mark the contents lying there in wait for Morgan's touch.

Above waist height the car's transparent. Domed and arching overhead, the sweep of glass collects the sunshine of his passage through the land. That glass is never dulled. An ionized field, a dust precipitator, works to clean the glass; at night its static charge leaves trailing flecks of biting blue behind.

Day or night, inside or out, this car gives off a splendor as it goes.

Toward that end was it built, not merely to impress a random watcher who might note its flight, but even more to satisfy the Morgan riding in it. Going to a university, toward his year of obligation, Morgan feels an anguish at the loveliness he must forsake upon arriving. That loveliness remains a constant in his memory, reminder of rewards awaiting his return. And it works. Morgans keep in mind the splendor of the journey to their undesirable posts. It helps to hold them faithful to their charge. If all goes well, that train awaits their outward journey, too.

All had gone well for Harold Stassen, the Morgan sent to Urban U. And now he revels in the luxury forsaken for his year in hell. He celebrates. His car is stocked with delicacies according to his taste. The car hums through the countryside, a hurtling beer truck. Behind each inlaid panel, no matter what insignia is carried there, are racks and rows of Meisterbrau. Not a modern substitute or imitation. The real thing. Meisterbrau.

Before the train had traveled eighty miles from Urban U., Morgan was half drunk.

Jackie was so taken by the passing landscape that she bubbled effervescently.

Only Kiley sat immobile, calm, and poised, and careful to display his unexcitement.

They sat in swivel chairs along the center axis of the car, drinking in the blue sky, cirrus clouds, brilliant sunshine beaming down on them. Morgan's chair was near the rear, faced forward. Jackie sat midcar, swinging one way, then the other, eager not to overlook a single sight they passed. At the front of the car, Kiley sat facing the rear. Their respective positions, the chairs they had chosen for themselves, mark an appropriate symbolism; life has its own artfulness.

"See it? That tower? Did you see it?" Jackie pointed behind them and appealed to Kiley for confirmation.

He smiled at her delight and nodded. "Looked like a silo with a bulb on top."

"Not a silo. Whoooo! How'd I know that word?" Morgan bounced eagerly in his chair but was careful to hold his bottle upright. "Haven't heard that word from anywhere. Must of read it. That's it. Read it somewhere. 'Silo,' building for storing animal food, right?"

"Right. When I was a boy—"

"Power tower, not a silo. That's what's running the train, you know? Broadcast power. Salvation of the world, all the economy based on it, problems all went pffft! Simple little thing like broadcast power. That bulb's the transmitter."

"It was pretty all the same," Jackie said. Too many explanations would spoil the fairyland she saw outside.

"Pretty? *Gorgeous!* Broadcast power, and no more pollution, no more poverty—I tell you, gorgeous!" Morgan rose and swayed in time to the music he nearly heard.

"Better sit down," Kiley said. "You'll hurt yourself. And we can do without the fairytales. No more pollution? I know better than that. I'm still sore from wearing those noseplugs."

"Here! *Here*, no pollution. Not back *there*. Not at the U. The forcefield keeps it bottled in where it belongs. Same thing as the field, broadcast power. Both work the same. But let me tell you, when I was a boy it was nothing like this." He pointed at the passing farmlands. "Skies were something awful, like in the U. Took years for it to go away, or settle, whatever happened. Now it's all locked up safe in the U. All the problems, locked up safe. When—huh!" The train lurched into a curve and threw Morgan against the glass wall. He slid to the floor and lay laughing.

"Let me help." Jackie pulled him to his feet and guided him back into a chair.

He depressed an ebony inlay shaped like a hand of bananas. The panel swung open, and he replaced his spilled bottle of Meisterbrau.

"Is it all like this?" Jackie asked.

On their left, between small mounded snowbanks, ran a trickling stream. Beyond it but short of the forests that capped the high hills in the distance stood the buildings of a farm. They looked historical, classical in design: white square house, squat and shuttered; red barn larger and gabled; small red outbuildings apparently used as storage sheds. The winter fields held a light cover of snow; a fringe of ice clung to the creekbank beside the sparkling water. To their right, at some distance from the train track, a small village marked a widening of the highway noticeable only because of the village itself.

Kiley thought the village looked deserted, no smoke from any chimney, and no traffic evident, though distance might have hidden that from sight. "Anyone live there?" he asked.

"Sure. Why not? Live where you want, even out here in the farmies," Morgan said. "Lots of people out here. But not me! Wait till we hit Washington. There's a city! Beautiful marble, thick forests. No place else in the world, not for me."

"What I meant was, I don't see any smoke. If people live there, they have to heat their—"

"See? You're still doing it. You think like my grandpa. Never understood, either. Broadcast power! Think about it. Electric heat, no smoke. I tell you, everything solved. May even write a book about it. Call it, *University and What It Gave Us*. Here's to my book." He hoisted his bottle.

For the first time since leaving the university, Jackie wore a puzzled frown. "I knew back in Montana it was like this, but I thought the East—"

"Everywhere. The whole country. Isn't it great? These people can't appreciate it, but let them spend some time in that hole back there, where we were, *then* they'll know. If you had a choice, where would you go? Here? Or some blackass university?"

"I had a choice," Jackie said. "That's why—"

"More fool, you. I've got a choice, too. And you see me taking it. Washington, where a man can grab the power handle. I *did* my tour." He leaned back and beamed at the light shining through his sweating bottle.

A heavy silence settled over them. Only the rush of the wind outside marked their passage, that and a hint of Debussy brushing near their consciousness.

It was Jackie who wouldn't let the subject die. "If the university's so awful, why are you involved?"

"*Was.* Was involved. There's the good of it. *Was* involved. Why? Somebody has to, that's why. Let the incompetents handle things and the whole system would collapse in a minute. Picture Haller running anything!" He grinned at his bottle and began to hum a secret tune.

"Nobody I know tells it your way." Jackie was plaintive.

Bees swarmed in Kiley's ears—the whole conversation confused him, shook the foundations of some certitude he couldn't identify. All he really knew was that Morgan was threatening his future.

"Who? Who else?" Morgan said. "Think they know? That's the beauty. Let them play at running things. Whatever happens inside doesn't matter. Forcefield. It's the final solution."

Kiley flinched as memory underlined the phrase. "I've heard that—"

"Doesn't matter. Perfect term, this time. Name the problems we had when you were young. All gone now. All of them."

"No," Jackie protested. "We still have to educate—"

"Rat it, honey! What the kids say, isn't it? *All,* I said. Crime? Always in the cities. Whoever got mugged out in the farmies? Take your blacks. Mostly in the cities before—did you know that? Now they're *all* there. Welfare leeches? Crooked politicians? In the cities. Slums? Riots? Polluters? Ghettos? Murder, rape, arson, looting, brainrot, incompetentdirtydegenerate. . . ."

Surprised at his own vehemence, Morgan paused for breath and heard himself. He poked out his tongue and stared crosseyed down at it. "Ummff! But that's all over now. Most of 'em in there would be scared green to see real clouds. It's been tested. All get terrified out from under the dome. Only reason you could come along"—he pointed at Jackie—"was you grew up outside. It's not so tough for you."

Kiley pictured himself facing a blank wall, nowhere to go, nothing to do. Impotence became more than a word to him. "If you've solved everything, what will I—"

"Solve, hell! Bottled up. It'll solve itself. Already happening." One of Morgan's hands floated in midair and marked time. He recited: "Birthrate in the cities, 10 percent of 1980 standard, Retardo and Antirect. Major crimes near zero. Nothing to steal, you see? Racial problems? None out here. Socialist agitators? All locked in where they belong." Suddenly he winked at them. The eye stayed closed. "You know the nice part? It's self-liquidating. Average life-span inside, 48.3 years, going down all the time. Great place for statistical data. Outside, emphysema nearly cured; studied in some U. population. Lung cancer? Sixty-four percent inside. Wonderful opportunity. Means cure soon available. All those people to—uh—study. By the time we open up, shut down the forcefields, major diseases licked, no black problem, no more—"

"What's that mean, 'open up'?" Jackie was on her feet, glaring at him.

Morgan waved a bored hand. He let the other eyelid fall. "Twenty, twenty-five years, make it. No more problems at all. Died out. Cheap at twice the price. Open the domes, turn 'em loose. Those who can take it. . . . Live to see it, maybe. Maybe me, I'll live to see it. Wonderful day. . . ." His head dropped to his chest and he slept.

The bottle fell from his hand and tumbled across the carpet, trailing foam. Kiley and Jackie watched it roll.

"He's drunk," Kiley said, too loud. He had to deny what he had heard. To accept it, even momentarily, raised a specter over his own future and denied his present authority. "Ignore him. He doesn't know—"

"He knows!" Hoarse, guttural.

In her tone he heard the recognition he was fighting. He couldn't let her—let himself—understand. "No, wait a minute. He's got an outsider's view. Don't let him bother—"

"How can I not?" She reached out and kicked the fallen bottle. "What if he's right? What if we've been helping—"

"Hey! Take it easy." He walked over and gently pushed her back into her chair. "Now you're worrying about motives. Do you think you're helping *anyone?* In any way? Would they get anything if it weren't for the universities? What does it matter *why* the U's there?"

She sat silent, unable to express the fears she felt.

"See? He's worked out an explanation he wants to believe. But he's only been there a few months longer than *I* have. What does he know about it? When we get back inside, we can—"

"You said it, too. 'Inside.' You *do* believe him."

Kiley let his anger surface. "I can hear, too. I've been listening to you since we left home. Do you know why you're not talking black any more? Think about it. Can you tell me why? No—not me. *Yourself.* Tell yourself. It's because we're outside."

He settled back in his chair and waited. It hadn't come out right. He knew the anger he showered on her had another target. But if what Morgan said about "inside" was right, there was nothing left to go back to. Morgan had to be wrong; Jackie had to be wrong. Kiley saw himself as the big frog in a pond gone dry.

She answered so softly that he barely heard her. "All your life, all you want to do is win arguments. Not discuss. You have to be right." She turned to stare into the twilight settling around them.

Every word that sprang to his lips was a contradiction, and therefore proof of her accusation. He choked them back and took refuge in blaming her femininity. She argued out of emotion, not logic. He might not be able to persuade her. Neither did he have to fall into her verbal traps.

He watched an ochre sun setting behind them. They would be

in Washington by morning. If she still felt disillusion, he could ask around. There was no need to accept Morgan's distorted view. He would find out for himself.

All Kiley had to do was ask. Would any congressman refuse to answer Robert Kiley? Not likely.

42

"HE GOT Jensen killed. True or not?"

Thirty students stood shuffling their feet uneasily in the windy tunnel. Few of them responded. Fewer met Tricia Neely's glare.

She stood on an upended keg, and that eminence let her tower over Tyrone Floy beside her. Taller now than he, she used her advantage. To us, it may seem a small one. Anyone who knows Retardo will recognize the importance of something so merely physical as height.

"Why are you here?" she demanded. "Did he, or not?"

Heads nodded in silence, and Tyrone felt his palms break sweat. His lieutenants, all thirty cell-leaders, had gathered for the trial. All knew that an incompetent general is worse than none. Whatever came of Tricia's calling him out, the children huddled in this echoing cavern would carry the news away with them. Throughout the university, individual cells waited for the result of the trial. And Tyrone knew how precarious his position had become.

He said, "I hear you. Jensen's dead. Do you want me to say it's my fault? Done. Now what—"

"That's not enough!" She smiled as if to soften the sting in her comment. There was little friendliness in the smile.

"Want to know why?" He disliked having to crane his neck to return her stare. She was upstaging him. "I admit it was a mistake. Too much depending on the ratting machinery, is that what you want to hear? Done. Next time will be different. I've been checking—"

"Next time, one of *us*? Wasn't Jensen enough?" Her smile grew feline, and the tip of her tongue flicked in pleasure as she toyed with him.

The children murmured.

"Do you want to listen?" Tyrone heard his voice cracking but couldn't prevent it. "I said, I've been checking on Fat Ethel, the night guard on Exit East. She's got a boy at Child Care who—"

"No! We *don't* want to listen. We'll be talking this garbage till security outs a couple more of us."

"Hey!" One voice.

That single agreement clawed at the sand Tyrone felt slipping beneath his feet.

"The rest of you?" Tricia demanded.

"Hey!" Several more, this time.

"Rat it!" Tyrone shouted. In the silence that followed he took a breath, watched Tricia daring his commitment with her eyes, and had the answer.

"Done," he said. "But she called *me*, true?"

"Hey!" From thirty straining throats. They circled closer in anticipation.

"Back off," he said. "She challenged me, I decide the way it is. My weapons." He faced her and dared a contradiction.

She shrugged. "Opensky."

"Then hear it. Tricia and I, in there." He pointed along the tunnel to the alcove where they had questioned Kiley. "One of us comes out, and we dump this garbage, agreed?"

They nodded, and Tricia dropped lithely off the keg to trot away down the tunnel ahead of Tyrone. He walked with as much dignity as he could muster. It may have fooled his lieutenants. He was now taller than she.

Murmuring voices followed him into the ill-lit alcove.

She stood, hands on hips, confident and waiting.

Her gaze told him that persuasion was useless. His thumb split the pressure seam down the front of his gray coverall. He shrugged out of it and let it drop to the floor, then motioned for her to do as much.

With her head cocked warily to one side, she did. She stepped away from him for the instant when her arms were trapped by the falling coverall. Then she faced him, arms folded beneath her firm, high breasts. "What's it to be?"

He stood immobile, tasting her lithe body with his eyes. "There's only one reason we even thought about Kiley coming in with us. We said, 'Who'll listen to kids?' Wasn't that it?" He stepped cautiously toward her.

Nodding, she backed away in a semicircle. She poised on the balls of her tiny feet and grew more catlike with each sinuous, coiling move of her tense retreat.

"You didn't call *me* out. You were cloud-mouthing little Tyrone, some kid you used to know. That's not me, is it?

"Well, is it?" His manhood rising, he stepped closer.

She backed into the darkness more quickly.

But not before he had seen the smile she tried to hide.

Her sudden dash for the alcove entrance fooled neither of them. He caught her easily in one sweeping arm and drew her back into the darkness.

It would be easy to misunderstand the next few minutes as rape. Call it sex instead. Or love. The differences do matter: rape denies a human dignity, sex affirms it, love creates it.

Neither of them raped the other, though both asserted something in the act.

"Fade to black" is sometimes commentary.

Watching would deny them dignity, as Retardo will have done. Fade to black.

43

AIMED TOWARD a rising sun, Morgan's train car plunged downward into blackness. Kiley and Jackie had spent the night in fitful sleep; since dawn they had avoided conversation, both careful not to utter the antagonism that hovered in the air between them. A new darkness swallowed them both, and the snoring Morgan, each of the three now alone. Slowly the glass dome overhead glowed to brighten the hurtling car with a soft, amber light. They shot through a tunnel under the Potomac.

At tunnel's end they popped into a terminal. The train stopped. And confusion began.

Before either of them could speak, the car doors split open to admit a small squad of uniformed men. In scarlet-and-green splendor, epaulets fluttering, white shakos nodding, six men entered. Their black boots shone like patent leather. Two of them carried a stretcher, rolled Morgan onto it, and left. All Morgans arrive in Washington drunk. With power, if not with Meisterbrau.

Two other men picked up the baggage and carried it out. The remaining pair delayed a moment, then motioned for Kiley and Jackie to follow.

"Where are you—?" Kiley found himself talking to a broad scarlet back. Shrugging, he trailed along, Jackie beside him.

Unconsciously, he timed the shuffling scrape of his ceramic clogs to the clump of marching boots.

They were led to an elevator and ascended into daylight as the elevator shot up through a transparent shaft mounted outside the building. It was their first look at our nation's new capital.

In the distance, perhaps two miles to the south, cream and glistening in the bright sunlight, rose the Washington Monument.

Buildings near it sparkled and glittered as if cleaned for the occasion, pools of light flickering in the forest. Kiley's chest swelled at the welcome laid out before his ascending feet. He felt Jackie's hand slip into his, then jerk away as she recognized what she had done.

She still hadn't spoken to him.

No one in the elevator spoke. Recollections of the Washington he had known crept up on Kiley, and he peered down at the greenery below: a forest, literally. Conifers, mostly, but here and there the gnarled fingers of an oak or elm or bare cherry tree reached into the winter sky. Paths of white gravel traced random curves through the manicured wilderness. Washington had become a picnic grounds, a setting for an Easter egg hunt, or the reconstructed archetype of virgin America.

Or deserted. He couldn't tell which.

The doors hissed open and the silent pressure of nodding shakos urged Jackie and Kiley into a huge room, carpeted with red, white, and blue stripes. The door closed, and they were alone.

We can assume that the Hebrew children, about to enter that fiery furnace, talked together. There are times when self-sufficiency is impossible. Jackie knew the feeling.

"What do you think?" she asked.

"Somewhere between impressive and depressing," he said. He dragged a clog through the thick-pile carpet and watched the nap crackle with static. "At least they're making us feel at home." He pointed across the blinding expanse of carpet at their bags—and Jackie's Christmas-gift umbrella—tumbling through a hinged panel onto the floor.

"But what do we do next?"

"Wait and see, I guess. Or try room service." He looked around for a phone but saw none. A mound of white fur sat in the center of the room—bed or couch, he couldn't tell. Beside it lay several footstools shaped like black spaniels lolling on the floor. The far wall was polarized glass, dark at this distance under the impact of the bright sunlight outside. He could see himself and Jackie reflected in it as two drab spots in the midst of all the color. A dozen-odd chairs in fluorescent hues circled the couch in ranked precision; each form-fitting plastic scoop teetered on a slender chrome pedestal. The left wall gleamed milk-green, a ten-by-thirty-foot triveescreen, and the right wall contained a hologram of a pale prune wearing a fringe of kinky gray curls. Kiley swerved toward it as he crossed to the window wall. Closer, he recognized it as the bust of some wizened old man. He read the chrome plate at the bottom of the frame: THE PRESIDENT, it said. On a shelf jutting from the wall beneath the hologram lay a pair of toothbrushes atop a chrome tray labeled "Take

Me." Each toothbrush was inscribed "Compliments of Nixon House."

Jackie pointed at the hologram. "One of the Presidents?"

"One of them."

She followed him to the window.

Here, opposite the elevator wall of the hotel, the view gave onto a reservoir on the left and—directly before them—a series of progressively smaller buildings reaching away like descending steps toward a wide band of forest a mile distant. The nearest building, topped by a fifty-foot-high neon emblem of a roasted chicken above crossed ax handles, bore a sign that read, "Maddox House."

Kiley started to ask, but choked on the idea.

Before he could formulate a harmless question, the wall behind them opened to admit Morgan. He seemed chastened. Sober, and sober. His chins covered his greasy collar as he shuffled through the plush carpet in deep thought. He had unpleasant news to share.

It was most unpleasant for him. Only moments before he had climbed from the stretcher, revived by a whiff of oxygen and a shot of Meisterbrau neutralizer, into a disappointment. Not only had bringing Kiley along earned him less congratulation than he had expected; the whole idea horrified his section chief in the Bureau of Budget Control. Their exact conversation is unimportant. All that matters is the result, which Morgan will try to temper as he can. He had expected fanfare and now faced anticlimax. Slinking toward them through the garish room, he was a sad, wasted little man. Not at all the self-possessed authority he had seemed in his office at the university. His baggy pants and slumping gait made him seem a circus clown, spreading cheer by contrast to the burdens showing through his own depressing mien.

"Why not tell us about it?" Jackie suggested. That's the way she is.

Morgan tried to square his shoulders and heroically managed a lopsided shrug. "Fine. All fine. Trouble is, it's a busy time here right now. Congress in session and all that. Understand?"

Yes, they said. They understood. They lied, of course.

"Where do we go from here?" Kiley asked. In imagination he

conjured up visions of receptions, fetes, and scores of dignitaries filing past to shake his hand.

Morgan slumped to the mound of fur and settled into its billowing softness. "Hard to say. I'm going to be busy at the . . . with the. . . . Very busy the next couple days. Budget hearings, and all. But you've got the trivee. Just make yourselves at home."

"Aren't we going with you?" Jackie tugged a fuscia chair close to the couch and dropped into it. She bent low enough to catch his eye.

Kiley stood watching, still lost in reverie.

"I don't think so. There's been a slight mix-up. Maybe in a day or two—"

"But they'll want to talk to Bob, won't they? What about—"

"That's mainly what they *don't* want." Morgan struggled to his feet to avoid her bewildered look. Several deep breaths did nothing to restore his confidence. "Well. Why not wait and see what happens? Your bedrooms are right through there, each side of the holo." He pointed at the Nixon wall, then made his escape.

As the door closed behind him, Jackie spun around. "That doesn't make any sense! After we came all this way?"

When Kiley refused to get excited, she took her irritation to the trivee screen and punched for room service on the panel Kiley hadn't seen before.

The screen overpowered them with light, and a five-times life-sized woman's face crooned, "Yes, Mr. President?"

"Um, well, no. This is Doctor Muller. I wanted to know—"

"Yes, President Muller?"

"Why do you keep saying that? All I wanted was some information. How far are we from the Capitol, here? Can you get us a cab?"

"Sorry, President Muller. Travel is not authorized." The woman smiled. Each tooth was two inches long. "Would you like to see a menu?"

"We want to look around. You didn't understand. Can you have a cab waiting for us—"

"Sorrreeee, President Muller. All university presidents are asked to wait in their suites until called for."

Jackie turned her frustration to Kiley, who had nothing to suggest.

"Listen, will you? I'm not 'President' anyone. I'm Doctor Jacqueline Muller, from Urban University. And this is Robert Kiley, here with me. Mister Kiley would like to leave the hotel."

"Sorreee, President Kiley. All university presidents are asked to wait in their suites until called for. Would you like to see—"

Jackie punched the screen blank and stood shaking her head. "Just like a recording. Damn! I don't think she ever *heard* of you!"

"If you really want to leave, why not walk out? We're not prisoners, after all."

He pushed the call button. The elevator arrived and its doors opened to admit them.

They *were* prisoners, of a sort, or should have been—prisoners of habituation, of conditioning that would keep most university presidents safely on call. But how could the hotel staff know that anyone from "inside" would dare to walk abroad under opensky? Kiley might claim that his determination and self-confidence let him enter the waiting elevator. In fact, it was simple ignorance.

44

TOGETHER, dressed once more, Tyrone and Tricia stepped out of the darkened alcove. A cresting murmur of disappointment met them.

"Before anyone starts wasting time, let me say—it's settled." He looked at her and hid a smile at the tired nod she offered. The waiting faces, an aura crackling in the air told him that now was the time. He suddenly knew with knife-edged clarity. Now was the time to persuade the others, before his tension and uncertainty returned to interfere.

"I tried saying it before. The reason we didn't make it outside the other peem was, we've been thinking too much like them." His gesturing thumb pointed overhead toward an enemy he didn't need to name. "*People!* That's what's opensky. People. Not those garbage machines *they* depend on. Will you listen?"

Tricia backed him up. "He's the man. We listen, true?"

"Hey." Half-hearted but willing.

"Done, then." Tyrone paused to get it right. He had to lead from strength. "One month. No more. If I don't have you outside in a month, out me."

"Ty!" Tricia snatched at his arm.

He jerked free. "No more fucking off! Hear it. If I don't have you free in a month, I'm dead." He felt his legs trembling but saw in their faces that he had them. Commitment. Lay it all on one bet.

The circle inched nearer. A few of them dropped into a crouch and hugged their knees, shivering.

"By ourselves? Without any Fac?" The long-haired boy Kiley had nicknamed Willis during the abortive class session pushed his way to the front. "No trouble now, Ty. Only asking."

"By ourselves. You've been sucking around Fac so long, and you still don't know what they're about?"

Willis stiffened. "I don't need any of—"

"Okay. I'm wrong. Only that whole 'honors' garbage of yours gets me windy sometimes. Maybe you like it too much the way things are now. Which way are you going? Nobody's half a virgin."

"Ty?" Tricia tried placating. "All it means is he's good. Ain't so? He's got Fac fooled thinking he's with them. And remember that class. He almost drove Kiley back to us."

"'Almost' gets nobody free. But no offense." Tyrone tensed a forefinger and snapped himself in the groin.

The choking laugh that burst from Tricia drew smirks. Willis blushed.

"Done, then. Here's where we go." Tyrone's pause was only half for effect. Slowly, he turned to meet each eye before continuing. "Starting tomorrow ame, tell your people, nobody works. I want every class dumped on, out the power on any campus-center building you can, plug the subways, strip batteries from the cabs—in general, all the garbage we got. *But,* only at campus center. I want Security in there, away from the ducts."

"Point?" Willis asked.

"Coming. When we've got them focused on campus center, start your people moving toward the ducts. Within a week, I want a thousand off the streets, disappeared."

"They'll check the ducts, number one," a gangling black girl interrupted.

"We'll keep moving. They haven't pinned us in here yet, have they?"

"Hey."

"But, one thousand? Against all of them?" Willis protested. "That's nothing. We'll be outnumbered so—"

"Listen, boy. Don't give me numbers. It's not how strong your pressure is. It's where you apply it." Tyrone paused for objections, but no one else spoke.

"'sky, then. And I'm after Fat Ethel's urban. Then we'll—"

"Out him?" Tricia asked.

"No killing. Not yet. For now, let's try and use him. Fat Ethel might come around, if we get her boy clear of Child Care and in with us."

"What's it mean, 'no killing'?" a squat boy leaned forward to ask. The fire in his eyes explained his question.

"It means you and I mix, if I hear of it. At least till I say."

"And you don't want the man down on you." Tricia rolled her eyes and brushed dancing fingertips over her small breasts.

"Hey!" some shouted, before catcalls and laughter drowned them out.

Tyrone smiled and let the laughter die away. "Have fun now. But try this one—some of us won't get outside, you know that?"

"Aww, Ty. We're all—"

"Rat it! Remember Jensen. You know what burned meat smells like? I promise you, the roaches were on him before we were fifty feet away. No! You!" He grabbed Willis by the arm and spun him around. "Don't turn away from that, not even in your head. If you don't think they'll out any one of us, I don't want you here. You think this is some game? You think any one of them will give up what he's got, just on our asking? You think they'll treat us like kids when the crunch comes?

"Well, do you?"

Willis snatched free and stood sulking for a long moment before he answered. "Sheet, man! It ain no sense studyin on 'em mothahs. It's us bloods gon—"

Tyrone's punch caught him high on the cheek and sent him sprawling into the front rank of the crowded circle.

"I, mean, this! Hear it!" He glared at all of them, prodding the fallen Willis with one toe as he spoke. "The next time *anyone* comes at me with that 'black' talk, I'm getting me a handful of crotch." He raised his right hand tensed as a claw and slowly, deliberately, turned to display it. "You think Retardo's slowing you down some? I'll make a few permanent sopranos, or watch you bleed to death in front of me. And you, *boy!*" He kicked Willis in the groin. "Tricia says you're real good. Got the Facs all cloudy, think you're special, right? To me—"

"Ty! Enough!" Tricia tugged at his arm but he tossed her aside.

"It's *never* enough. And it's not 'black' I'm talking about. I don't *see* black, I don't *know* it, I won't *hear* it. I'm black. You think that matters? Any of you? Tricia's not. Does that matter?

"Here's what matters!" He whirled and hooked one hand in the collar of a girl's gray coverall. He ripped it free to her waist.

Instinctively, in reflex, she crossed her arms and bent low to conceal herself.

Tyrone touched her shoulder gently. "Love? Do you know what I'm saying?"

She nodded and slowly stood erect. Her hands fell to her sides. She stood exposed. Flat-chested, youthful, childlike. Blinking quickly, she tried a smile that failed.

"Tricia?" Tyrone held out a hand to her.

She dropped her coverall and stood in contrast.

"That's what matters," he whispered. He put his arm around the young girl's shoulders. "Tricia? Stay and talk to them about it. Make it clear. Anyone who can, dress like Kiley from now on. It's the best cover we've got. Blend in. Look like the others. But know this—it won't be for long."

He led the young girl away, whispering to her.

45

The ELEVATOR control panel bore only three buttons, labeled "Suite," "Ground," and "Terminal." Kiley led Jackie from the elevator into the street and glanced back at the façade of Nixon House— on it, a series of transparent tubes of different lengths, a separate elevator to each suite. The hotel looked like a huge cathedral organ whose sparkling pipes reached up in sunlit brilliance.

"They mean it," Kiley said with some surprise. "If all the U. presidents are inside right now, they'll never see one another. Private entrances."

Jackie was too occupied with her own suddenly shaky nerves to answer. She stood shivering in the crisp air and stared upward into a blue abyss whose very vacancy nearly hypnotized her. She wrenched her eyes away and complained, "What's wrong with the heat? Why is it . . . ?" She heard and understood her own comment. It was habituation speaking; accustomed to the thermostatically regulated life within the university, she found it an effort now to recall any other experience. They hadn't dressed for opensky. That accounted for part of her trembling. But not all of it.

Kiley threw his jacket around her shoulders and pointed across the street. Near the entrance to Maddox House a black in scarlet livery stood watching them.

They crossed over and Kiley asked, "Can you get us a cab?"

"Yassuh boss. Ah sholy gwine do it." He flashed a toothy grin and tugged at his forelock. His kinky hairpiece slid down over his eyes. With one white-gloved hand he pushed his hair back into place, muttering. His black forehead sported several pale streaks. His white glove was stained with burned cork.

"Yawl guests heah, boss? Ah kin fetch a boy to take yawl down to deh ole cullud paht a taown, if yawl want."

Kiley felt himself part of a practical joke. He looked around to see who else might be involved. It wouldn't have surprised him to see Shirley Temple tap-dancing along the sidewalk.

They were alone on the street. He realized then that he had seen no traffic yet, no cars, cabs, trucks, buses, bicycles, not even pedestrians.

"Why are you painted up like that?" Jackie asked.

With offended dignity, the doorman said, "Ain't yawl nevah seen no culluds 'fore? Ouah visitors usual wants to see what the old-timey—"

"We're not tourists," Kiley interrupted. "I'm Robert Kiley."

"That's true," Jackie said. "He is that, all right." She giggled in a shrill voice and stared at the ground.

"Maybe yawl's agents, checkin on how 'is pore ole niggah doin his job?"

"I don't know what you're—"

The man leaned close to hiss, "Get the hell out of here! It ain't bad enough wearing this goddamn grease, now I got to stand here talking to you two. The tour's coming by any minute, and they're going to want to see a nigger at work. Just flake off, will you? Want to cost me my job?"

On cue, a jitney rounded the corner and pulled up before Maddox House. A dozen well-dressed people debouched with cameras already aimed. A guide herded them toward the doorman.

Kiley and Jackie stepped aside and pantomimed conversation. She still shivered. Without his coat, he could feel the chill seeping in. The knot of tourists puzzled him. Repeated glances at them did little to clear away his confusion, until he noticed their dress. As unlikely as it seemed, they reminded him of 1973—their clothes, attitudes, the very way they walked and stared at the doorman and the gilt front of the hotel, was familiar. As if time hadn't passed, for them. They were strange in their very familiarity—oxfords, top-coats, scarves, fur coats, purses, cameras. He had grown accustomed to noticing novelty, but nothing about them had changed. They looked undistinguished.

We might be in that very group of tourists, when the time comes. And we certainly won't appear strange to one another.

But Kiley was different.

One of the women in our group, a woman swaddled in leopard-skin furs and wearing a cultured pearl headband, interrupted the guide's comments to ask, "What about that one?" She pointed at Kiley.

He might have been a man from Mars. In his shirtsleeves, hair-less, teetering atop his glass blocks, shivering in the chill air, and standing aside as if waiting for ———.

"What's that one do?"

Jackie giggled again. "Do you know who this is? He's Robert Ki—"

"Shhh!" he cut her off. It embarrassed him to hear his name thrown into their midst. Though he had done it himself, only moments earlier, in her mouth his name was less password than accusation. To be named is to be defined. The trembling that threatened him more each second would grow worse with that definition.

The tourists never knew that they had seen Robert Kiley Himself. They wouldn't have cared, anyway.

The guide and doorman exchanged unconcerned shrugs.

"He's probably one of the employees. Now if you'll—"

"But look at those feet."

Our group abandoned the minstrel and gathered around Kiley.

Jackie seized his arm and pulled him away down the street. His swooping gait triggered laughter behind them, but they hurried around the corner of the hotel.

A street sign registered on Kiley's mind: Georgia Avenue.

Wordlessly, they started toward the Washington Monument, which reared above the forest before them.

For half an hour they scuffed along gravel paths through the artificial wilderness, at each fork bearing south. Trees of equal height, standing in geometric rows and patterns on each side, screened them from the brunt of the wind. Even so, they shivered as they walked. Patches of melting snow lay in shadow beside the path. Jackie stared at the ground and fought the impulse to glance up into the sky.

They guided themselves by glimpses of the monument showing through the trees at odd intervals. It began to change appearance for them. On the top was mounted a bulbous swelling, like the spire of a Russian church.

As they walked, Kiley tried to re-create in his mind the city of Washington he had known. The distance they covered, along with an indefinable sense of place that forced itself on him, gave him a mental map. Streets and intersections came back to him. Individual buildings showed themselves in imagination. Nixon and Maddox Houses apparently stood at the old site of Howard University. That name triggered others: Trinity College, Georgetown, Dunbarton College, George Washington, Catholic U.—many of them. Where had they gone? Shouldn't D.C. be a "university," too?

Clearly not, for whatever reasons. The clots of ghetto housing, the small businesses, the shops and arcades, the playgrounds, the whole tangled character of a community had disappeared. Now, so far as he could tell in his frigid wandering, Washington was nothing but forest and, in the near distance, flickering hints of marble buildings seen through the trees.

The woods ended, and they stepped out onto K Street. There was the White House; to the southeast, Independence Mall; to the southwest, the shining obelisk with its newly swollen peak.

Kiley recognized the bulbous cap. "Broadcast power," he said. "Like the silos we saw on the train."

Jackie might have been listening. She stood motionless and didn't answer.

"Down to the left. The Capitol's that way. If Morgan's really tied up in his budget hearings, it ought to be there.

"You all right?"

Jackie nodded listlessly and drew her coat collar tight about her neck.

"Well, I guess that's where we're headed," he said.

They never got there.

They had walked a block down Vermont Avenue when a klaxon broke the silence with its blatting protest. A squad of shako-topped guards burst into view from the White House lawn ahead, double-timing in cadence toward them.

Kiley whirled to judge the distance back into the cover of forest. Retreat was impossible. Several men in beige business suits stepped from the trees to saunter toward them, never looking directly at them but obviously closing in. One of the men read a newspaper as he walked. The others whistled or talked among themselves, in every way displaying unconcern while they bore down on Jackie and Kiley like automated insurance salesmen.

The scarlet-and-green-garbed juggernaut reached them first. The guards waved weapons and chanted something unintelligible.

The plain-clothes force approached from the rear.

Caught between mayhem and the methodical, Kiley felt like a hockey puck in a faceoff.

One of the shakos spoke first. "White House affair. They crossed the determinator. No pass. We'll handle it."

The man with the newspaper answered. "I don't think so. We're in 'hot pursuit.' Boundaries don't apply." He folded the newspaper and slipped it under his arm. He reached up to tip his beige homburg. "Miss? Sir? Will you come with us, please? But let me advise you of your rights. You have the right to remain silent. If you decide—"

"Can it, will you?" The man in the shako gave a hand signal, and his troops snapped to attention. "I have the duty to inform you that the President has ordered—"

"President? We are under direct personal orders from the Director!"

The plainclothesmen drew themselves to attention, or to its civilian equivalent, at the mention of that title.

Jackie and Kiley glanced from one force to the other.

"President!"

"Director!"

"Can we leave?" Jackie asked.

Kiley knew what she meant, though the tremor in her voice disturbed him.

"President!"

"Mr. Hoover!"

The guard spokesman's shako seemed to wilt. He backed away several steps and whispered to one of his men.

"That's right," the beige man reaffirmed. "Mr. Hoover. Now, will you please go back to whatever it is you people do?"

The resplendent guards milled for a moment, in their red and green whirling a kaleidoscope of traffic lights.

"All right, dammit! Attention there!" The guard commander wheeled and led them away.

"Forgive all the confusion," the beige man said. "Here." He flashed an official-looking card at them but snatched it away before Kiley could read it. "Please come with us."

"Why?" Kiley said. "What's this all about?" He looked at Jackie, afraid that she might use his name as a password again, but she stood mute.

"I must inform you that anything you say may be taken down and used in evidence against you. If you wish to be represented. . . ." His voice blurred into a triple-speed monotone. He turned his back and continued to recite as he walked away.

Kiley and Jackie followed. They were surrounded by the clean-cut young men, all with fresh haircuts, all in beige business suits, all wearing tense, unfriendly smiles. Like Ken dolls.

They sauntered. None of the escort looked at them. The man leading the way reopened his newspaper and began to read. Once he walked into a lamppost, but his subordinates refused to notice.

Silently, they filed inside a sidewalk kiosk and walked down a flight of stairs. Three men entered one open car with Jackie; Kiley and three others sat in a second open car. They moved through subterranean semidarkness, till the front car suddenly darted into a branching tunnel; and Kiley watched Jackie being spirited away.

"What's that about?" he demanded. "Where—"

"I must inform you that anything you say may be taken down and used in evidence against you. If you wish to be represented. . . ."

Kiley debated reaching over to light the newspaper the beige man held up before his face as a screen. But he knew that the man at each elbow, no matter where they seemed to be looking now, would stop him. He didn't think he had any matches, anyway.

"Have you got a match?"

"I must informyouthatanything. . . ."

He was taken from the car, along a corridor, up an escalator, and urged into an office. Embedded in the huge mahogany office door were scores of rhinestones that spelled out, in foot-high letters spaced diagonally down the polished wood, THE DIRECTOR.

The beige man reached up to tip his homburg and poked himself in the eye with the newspaper. None of his subordinates laughed. They continued to smile.

The door closed.

"Sit, please."

Kiley flinched and looked for the source of the metallic voice that surrounded him. A single chair stood in the center of a large, empty room. Tile floors, institutional gray walls, no windows or doors except the door through which he had entered, and the inside of that was painted gray as well.

"Sit, please. To your right."

It sounded like a man talking under water. The comment told Kiley he was being observed. He sensed unseen eyes crawling over his skin. Cautiously, he eased himself into the wooden chair. It was fastened to the floor.

"This will be brief. You may ask questions when—"

"Are you the Director?"

"—I've finished. A mistake has been made. Your Morgan-Stassen incorrectly assumed that certain congressmen might wish to interrogate you. That is not the case. You may return to your hotel until such time as the new Morgan arrives to escort you back to your university. Is that clear?"

The wall in front of Kiley was blank and featureless. He had nowhere to direct his gaze, as if he were sitting in a dentist's chair. The chair he now perched uncertainly on lacked arms, or padding, or any concession to comfort. And the seat seemed tilted; he kept sliding forward and had to brace himself. His clogs found no purchase on the polished tile floor.

"Is that clear?"

"Yes. I—well. No, dammit! It's not. What have you done with Doctor Muller?"

"Your—uh—'companion' has been returned to the suite, for her own welfare. As Morgan-Stassen should have understood, you people from inside are constitutionally unable to function at large. Most become catatonic at once. A few hours more and the girl might have been driven psychotic."

"She'd fit right in, wouldn't she? Listen. Where are you? And *who* are you?"

"I am the Director."

The next question refused utterance for a long moment, but Kiley dredged it up and forced himself to speak. "They, those men out there. They called you 'Hoover.' Not . . . it's not. . . . Is your name J. *Edgar* . . . ? I'm sorry. I know—"

"Yes."

Kiley's tenuous grip let go, and he crashed to the floor. The sudden embarrassment only made him angry. He scrambled to his feet and shouted, "That's crazy! Fifty years ago you were . . . he was—"

"Quiet! Fifty years ago, young man, you were dead."

"Does that mean you went through the same process?"

"People are named for what they do. Jack the Ripper, Apple Annie, William Shakespeare, Red Ryder—even Stassen is called Morgan."

Kiley felt himself hip-deep in verbal quicksand. "Then, you're not *really* who they say."

"Of course I am. Everyone is."

"Now, wait. Wait a minute. Why did you get me in here? What's the connection? Are you saying it's because I'm Kiley?"

The long silence was more frightening than anything the chanting, burbling voice had said. Finally, the unseen speaker crackled, "What is a Kiley?"

"Me! I! Robert Kiley! The Kiley from Urban University."

"Hold one, please. That will be checked."

Again the silence pressed down on him. He closed his eyes as if limiting his senses would help him locate the voice when it spoke.

"Apologies, Doctor Kiley. I should have recognized the name."

Only then did Kiley take a breath. He slumped with relief and eased himself onto the chair. "Then you *did* want to see me."

"For what purpose, Doctor Kiley? Our records indicate that you were the subject of Combined U-Fed Project 162. A fortuitous proof of the feasibility of cryogenic preservation of a complex living organism. But the results of that project are filed. Toward what end would I wish to *see* you, as you put it? The records are eminently clear." Real bewilderment sounded through the burbling voice.

Kiley seized the chair seat with both hands and held on. "No, not that. I mean *The Kiley Proposal.* I drew up the plans for all your universities. My plans—"

"Pardon me, Doctor Kiley—"

"And it's *Mister* Kiley. Check your—"

"Mister Kiley. You have been misinformed. The University Governance Board, in conjunction with the Bureau of Budget Control, under authority of an Executive order, approved by national referendum, devised the welfare program you apparently allude to."

"But I *know* better!" Kiley insisted. "I've read both my books"—he bit his lip and sought a new opening. "Everyone at the university knows I'm responsible. They all—"

"Then they are wrong. But they are wrong about many things, so I advise you to disregard this particular instance of their being in error. Have we quite finished now?"

The room seemed brighter, the gray walls soothing rather than oppressive. One word hung glowing in the air before Kiley's glazed eyes: "responsible," a word—more, a concept—he had denied even in his most private self-criticism. And there it was, revealed and refuted. As simple as that. Just as he will have claimed all along.

He felt clean again, although until that moment he hadn't known that he felt dirty. "Then I'm *not* responsible."

"Of course you are. I imagine your books were consulted, if they were available. In which case, you share the credit with all—"

"But it's not 'credit'! It's blame. You don't know what goes on inside—"

"Blame, then. Really, Mister Kiley. I have little interest in your hair-splitting discriminations. To be frank with you, my lunch is getting cold. You were invited here as a courtesy, considering Morgan-Stassen's error in bringing you 'outside' in the first place. Now, you may return inside, and we will overlook what you've said."

"Said about *what?*"

There was no answer.

Kiley wanted to be angry, but couldn't. Any strong emotion requires an object on which to fasten it. The Director was in no real way an object.

Kiley slid from the chair seat.

The beige man was standing beside him.

"When did you come in?"

"Imustinformyouthat—"

"Oh, stick it."

He let himself be led from the room and back to Nixon House.

Jackie was there. Like a hummingbird she flitted constantly about the room, talking incessantly, hearing none of the pauses he offered in nonanswer to her rhetorical questions.

It took only a few minutes for him to understand. She was high. Excitement, relief, drugs, alcohol—he couldn't tell what had done it, but she was high.

That satisfied him. He needed privacy. Her condition gave him more real privacy than her absence might have; she drowned out everything about the garish room and left him to his thoughts.

They sat together on the mound of white fur and ignored each other.

At some later time he became sensuous again. Darkness had fallen; he saw stars freckling the night sky. He grew aware of the striped carpet, of his stiff neck, of sweat soaking his shirt where Jackie's head lay in sleep. Stretched out before his gaze, his clogs rested on one of the mock-spaniel footstools. Carefully, he eased Jackie's head off his shoulder and onto the couch. He picked up the footstool, held it aloft, inverted, and rubbed the ball of his thumb over the blunted claws.

"Stuffed," he said. "See? A real dog." He held it out to her and tapped the collar. " 'Checkers.' "

She tossed in her sleep and grunted.

He answered himself. "Sentimentality. It started with sentimentality."

46

THERE ARE DRAWBACKS to comfort and security. Lotus-eaters risk obesity. For two days, Bizads secure in their counting houses and Fac snug in their tape-filled studies didn't notice the quiet rebellion burgeoning around them. But like a watch dunked in honey, the university began to slow down. There was no sudden shock, no overt violence. Minor annoyances accumulated unchecked.

Howard Bengston was irritated when the power failed at the Stimucenter and a host of clamoring students gathered at his office door to beg for current.

Hobart Reid set several subordinates the task of clearing away debris piled atop the subway tracks at three separate campus-center locations. He knew nothing about the collapse of cab service. His position let him drive one of the few gasoline-powered trucks still operable within the university.

Ethel Pease was puzzled when Warren failed to appear for breakfast. She sat staring through the one-way window till the Department of Child Care dining hall emptied. If she had known whom to ask, she might have learned that, two days earlier, Warren hadn't returned from his class in Waxes and Polishes.

Doctor Ling Chiu died. It was simple heart failure and had nothing at all to do with the quiet revolution, but the conspirators immediately claimed responsibility—with Tyrone's permission.

In three Workring factories, furnaces were allowed to cool down. Less than 10 percent of the day crew showed up for work. Fac recorded the absences in their grade books, gave each student his daily A, and gathered in the Department of Foundry lounge. They expected to watch a film, sent from Washington, concerning carborundum. Someone had stolen the projector.

Carleton Floy knew what was happening. He had known for some time what his son was planning and was torn between parental concern and his sense of duty to the university. He tried to commit suicide by swallowing his entire supply of Retardo. Nearly one hundred capsules. Within minutes he vomited them up again, yet for two days his voice squeaked. His testes grew so inflamed and painful that, in order to get home from his office, he had to walk like John Wayne.

Tyrone moved his command post to Thirty-duct and smiled continually. He was pulling the temple down around them all. Something better would rise from the rubble.

Peter Clausewitz noticed nothing out of the ordinary.

President Philip Haller walked outside his house to find painted on the front door a wilting phallus. For several hours he tried to resign. No one would accept his resignation. Finally one of his nine houseboys—a Kiley-clad student in the Department of Domestic Services—suggested that he talk to Morgan.

And Urban U. was without a Morgan.

47

MORGAN SULKED. He saw ahead of him a full year of exile inside Urban U., and—no matter the cheerful advice so freely offered by Morgan-Stassen, whom he was relieving—he decided to detest every second of that year. He sat in the splendor of his private railway car and ignored the muted whispers at his back.

"Just get a good look. You'll see." Kiley pointed the length of the car at Morgan.

Jackie saw nothing special. That was part of what Kiley meant.

Morgan was older than either of them had expected, nearing sixty, if his appearance told the truth, and wore a yellow silk scarf around his scrawny neck. But for that single affectation, he might have been anyone's grandfather.

"If I understand the system, he's exactly wrong for the job," Kiley said. "Morgan's usually a young man. Someone trying to make a reputation. Isn't that how it works?"

"Far as I know."

"Then, either the system's breaking down, or they've quit worrying about Urban. Or maybe he's some sort of incompetent being punished for a mistake. Like being made ambassador to Liechtenstein. He's too old."

"Is it really punishment?" Jackie's question seemed formal and offered as a time-filler. Some people nod.

Kiley didn't expect a real answer from her. They had talked matters through well enough while waiting for this Morgan to collect them from Nixon House and shepherd them back "inside." Neither of them nursed many illusions now. Yet their shared understanding took form in differing attitudes. Frankly, Jackie's insight had preceded his. Even before reaching Washington she had lost hope over what they might expect to find awaiting them. The actual shock of recognition had left her burned out and listless. No matter what question Kiley posed to her now, she resorted to silence or terse cynicism.

"Drop it," she said. "It doesn't matter."

To Kiley, it did. Embarrassed to admit how swollen his ego had grown, and at his own futile attempts to rationalize away the truths that Jackie's instincts had so quickly uncovered, he now felt compelled to press beyond her mere understanding. Knowing was no longer enough. He had to do.

"What good will *he* be?" Disdain dripped from her voice and would have shamed anyone less withdrawn than the sulking Morgan.

"How do I know? But look at it this way. If we can keep him from getting too involved, we ought to be able to make some changes. Let's assume all he wants to do is keep the lid on. He's not out to make his mark. Give him a soft berth and we'll be okay. We can use him."

He waited for her support, but she sat silent.

"At least we can *try!*"

She shrugged. Forgiving Kiley's earlier arrogance was one thing; helping to foster more of it, toward whatever end, was another.

"I have to," he insisted. "Like it or not, some of that hell in there comes from me. That proposal of mine—"

"Isn't this breast-beating a little silly? For weeks you've been telling me how everyone misunderstood you. That proposal was something floating in the air, an idea whose time had come. And your name got linked to it. Isn't that the whole speech? What did I leave—"

"No! It's too easy that way. There's nothing wrong with my proposal, *the way it was written*. But look what happened: footnotes, editing, all the nonsense that's being laid at my feet. And what about the students? Are they free? Treated as adults? Allowed any say in what happens to them? You know damn well they're not! It's too easy for me to blame someone else for that. Like it or not, as far as anyone knows, I *am* responsible.

"I won't take Eichmann's way out. Something has to be done." He stood suddenly. "And he can help."

She watched him drag his chair down the length of the car and sit beside Morgan.

The two of them held that tableau, Kiley talking, Morgan withdrawn and nodding absently, until the train entered the university forcefield dome. They were home.

They left the car and went inside, passing Ethel Pease at the window of her control booth.

No one was there to meet them. Kiley raised his eyebrows in question. Actually, since he lacks eyebrows, he wrinkled his forehead. Jackie had no answer.

None of the electric cabs parked along the curb would start.

"What the hell is this?" Morgan asked.

Neither could tell him. Privately, both were trying to decide whether the air was really more fetid than they recalled. Perhaps the short visit outside had colored their perceptions.

"We can always walk," Kiley said.

They led the cursing Morgan through grimy streets to his office. The flickering green field overhead seemed to Kiley lower, denser, more oppressive at each stride.

48

CLAUSEWITZ SAT WAITING on the steps of Kiley House.

"Ah heah y'all come back. Is it fix up? Did we git pass them sen'turs?"

"Morgan can tell you better than I can. What's this about?" Kiley pointed at the trash strewn beside the curb. As far as he could see, heaps of garbage lay along the sidewalk, invitation to the rats that undoubtedly infested each pile already. Half the buildings in sight bore the same crudely painted legend: OUT RETARDO. GET A KILEY.

"It's kids fuckin off again, s'all. Nuffin special. What Ah'm ax you 'bout is—"

"Nothing special? Look around. None of the cabs work, the subway's tied up, garbage everywhere. And these signs." He pointed at one of them decorating the very wall of Kiley House. "All the way over here from Morgan's office we saw them. On every block. Do you know what it means?"

Clausewitz jumped to his feet and stood as tall as possible. Then he climbed one step higher to look Kiley in the eye. "Is you axin would Ah *read* somepin?"

"No offense," Kiley said. "But dammit, man! The whole place is falling apart, and you sit there worrying about the budget."

"Shouldn't we go inside?" Jackie asked quietly.

They followed her up to the third-floor apartment. Clausewitz tried to restrain his excitement but made a display of carrying some important news he wanted to share.

Neither the light nor the air conditioner was working. They found chairs in the pea-soup twilight.

"Now kin Ah tell you?"

"Anything," Kiley said.

"It's Presiden Hallah tryin to quit!" He waited for the news to sink in. His head swiveled back and forth as he weighed the effect of his announcement.

"I don't blame him," Jackie said. "I've been thinking of the same thing."

"No!" Clausewitz bounded to his feet. "Y'all still ain gittin it on. Wif Hallah out, we ain got no presiden. An some of us figure, you! Why not you?" He pointed a pale, trembling finger at Kiley. "You the man now, Brothah Kahley. It's lack a miracle, s'what Ah mean. We put yoah name up, an it's evah one them fuckin kids votes for you. Doan y'all see that? We gon. . . ."

The lights flared on to interrupt. The air conditioner clattered to life.

"See! Ah tole you wasn't nuffin. It's Fac out theah raht now, doin what them kids spoze be at. So 'is breakin down shit's all clean up. Think on it. You lemme put yoah name up, or either you do it yourself, one, an it's all set. Y'dig?"

Kiley fought the impulse to laugh aloud. It was as if he had never left. He had gone outside a hero, returned that same hero—as if nothing had changed. But then, here, nothing had. His new understanding wouldn't alter matters "inside." Clausewitz might even be making sense. If the name Kiley had value for anything other than decorating sidewalks, the plan could work. He looked to Jackie.

She wasn't bothering to fight her laughter. She chuckled openly.

"Sistah? Wheah youah head at? It's somepin goin down heah in which Ah ain dig. You think am Ah funny?"

"No. Not you," she sputtered through her delight. "Him." She waved a hand at Kiley. "The idea of him as president of this place. It's so right! If I didn't know you were serious, I'd explain the joke."

"Woman! You ain 'splain *nuffin* to me! Not the way you talkin." He spun to face Kiley. "Whass happen to her? She ain talk 'is Bizad shit when she done went off wif you. Is it anythin go down in Washington when—"

"We're both a little tired, that's all. Can't you understand? We had a rough couple of days." Kiley walked over and carefully guided Clausewitz to the door. "Give us some time to get settled. Check with us in the morning. She'll feel better then, and so will I."

"What 'bout the 'lection? Kin we put you in?"

"In the morning." He closed the door.

"Now." He walked over to Jackie and dropped to one knee beside her. Gently, he pried open the cupped hands behind which she was hiding. "Jackie? Stop crying. I. . . ."

A twinkle greeted him. Then she burst into laughter again. "Oh, wait. Wait a minute. That man!"

Kiley sat back on his heels and matched her infectious grin.

"That man! I was just thinking. He'll make you president, and I've got a job for him. He'd be a perfect doorman for that Maddox House." Her voice became more mocking, nearly bitter. "All he needs is the makeup." She reached out to tap him on the shoulder. "And thee, I dub President Kiley."

She grew suddenly sober. "It could be trouble, too. From what you said about the students who kidnapped you—"

"I know. All the power failures and the rest of it. They're through waiting. What I've got to do now is find them, before they really blow the lid off." He peered to see whether she might try to dissuade him.

"Do you know where to go?"

It was Kiley's turn to smile. "This isn't the scene I expected. Aren't you going to say, 'Be careful, sheriff'?"

"Oh, I guess not. You've always been careful enough. Remember. I know a few things about Robert Kiley."

"Even if you won't ask, I'll be careful. Is that what you mean? I wasn't cut out to be a hero. President, maybe. But nothing as important as an honest-to-god hero. I'll find them."

49

"Trust the students, and they will trust us."

Afterword, *The Kiley Proposal*

KILEY DID KNOW what to look for. Nearly all the students he had so far seen on the streets wore the costume. They were little Kileys. But the few who wore the gray coveralls did so for reasons obvious to anyone who knew what he was seeking: the coveralls concealed adolescence.

Three blocks from Kiley House he stopped a gray-clad girl. "Can you tell Tyrone I want to see him?"

She backed away with suspicion. "Sorry, Mis' Kiley. I don't know what you mean."

"No trouble, now. I only want to talk to him. I'll wait in the park, if that's okay." He watched her turn and run.

Twenty minutes later a cab picked him up on Skinner Avenue. The young driver refused to answer any questions. He dropped Kiley beside a roaring, gaping tunnel mouth near the base of the flickering forcefield, then drove away.

Filling his lungs with the foul air, Kiley dashed into the duct and through the whoosh of debris. Wind-driven sand bit at his cheeks, paper scraps circled his head as he ran. He darted into a side tunnel and paused to catch his breath, out of the force of the gale. There was that stench again.

A few yards ahead a huddled figure in gray motioned him closer and then walked off. Kiley followed through several branching tunnels until he understood that he was being routed through a maze. He would not be able to find his way back here again unguided. Worse yet, he might not be able to find his way out.

The roaring wind seemed always just beyond the stone wall on either side. At intersections he caught occasional glimpses of other furtive gray figures ducking for cover as he passed. All the tunnels looked identical. He assumed that he had covered the same few yards several times before his guide stepped through a fabric curtain into an alcove Kiley thought he recognized.

Tyrone was there. So was Tricia. Both seated in judgment behind a low table. Several other students wore bandanas as masks. Kiley managed to control the smile their appearance evoked—like desperados out of some film. The room was tiny. On one wall hung a blanket. A boy was hanging another beside it, over a large chart. Probably a table of organization, or a battle plan.

Kiley looked around for weapons but saw none. That meant nothing. He wasn't certain that he would recognize one, anyway. "Eversharp," he mumbled.

"Picking sides with the winner?" Tyrone asked. "It may be too late; you know that, don't you?"

Kiley sat in a chair facing them and tried to appear relaxed. He had come by choice; that fact alone gave him the edge in their conversation. It was Tyrone's turn to be puzzled. And Kiley had to keep it that way, at least until he determined how best to proceed.

"Have you calculated your losses?" Kiley asked.

"Zero. How's that? No losses." Tyrone draped an arm around Tricia's shoulders and pulled her close. "Half of them don't know what's going on. By the time they do, it will be all over."

"Oh? What does that mean? What's the end result?"

Tricia answered. "No reason for you to know, is there? You'll find out when the rest do. Why did you want to see us?"

"I don't think I do. I asked to see *him*. Isn't he the leader?"

"No chance, Kiley," Tyrone said. "We're in family here. We don't split up that easy. Say your piece."

"I came to help."

Tricia laughed. "Sure. Only you waited till we didn't need you. Why should we bother? Everything's working—"

"You'd better bother!" he hissed at them. "You haven't a chance in hell!" He tried to cram real anger into his voice. He could hear himself acting and hoped they wouldn't notice. They didn't really know him. He had to depend on that.

It was working. Even those students walking idly around in contrived nonchalance paused. A small boy seated on a box in the corner looked ready to cry. Though no one met Kiley's glare, they were all listening.

"That's better. Do you know what they'll do when they understand? Do you think they'll take this without clamping down? You can't fight them all. Be sensible. This is suicide. When they—"

"Rat it, Kiley." Tyrone's voice sounded bored, but he sat stiff and straight with tension, his dissembling apparent. "They're so busy worrying about who's going to keep the factories running, or the food coming, that we can do anything we like. Your friend Clausewitz—"

"Not them, *boy!* Outside! That's 'they.' The ones outside. You're not a pimple on white man's ass to them!"

Tricia sprawled over the table reaching for him. Two students grabbed Kiley's arms and jerked him roughly to his feet.

"Ty? Say it! Lemme out him. Now!" The boy twisted Kiley's arm and forced him to his knees. The stone floor bit into his flesh.

"Hold it!" Tyrone snapped. Slowly, he stood and walked around the table. He cupped his hand under Kiley's chin and tilted his face up. He stared a long moment in silence before saying, "Let him go.

"I mean it. Now! Back off."

Kiley's captors released him. He returned Tyrone's stare and tried to ignore Tricia. She held a small knife in one trembling hand.

When Tyrone spoke it was in measured, curious tones. "What's the game, Kiley? You're not that stupid. Why the insults?"

Kiley brushed small bits of stone from his knees and straightened his stiff back. "Good. Maybe you are the right one. But your friends here—they fly off the handle pretty fast. Can you make it with people like that?"

"I don't like being tested, if that's what you mean."

"Ty? Let me do him." Tricia still trembled with anger.

"'sky. Not to worry. Well? Answer me, Kiley. Are you trying to get some attention? You've got it. Now it better be good. I'm not 'boy' to you. Now, or ever. Believe it!"

"Hey!" the watching children shouted.

"Okay. But you are to them. When you say 'they' can't do anything, you're not thinking straight. Who's your enemy? Fac? Bizad? Haller? Get smart. Maybe they're handy; you can *see* that opposition. But I've been outside. That's where the trouble is. Not here."

"Nothing. We heard all—"

"Listen, dammit! I mean it. I spent a couple of days in Washington, with Morgan. You must know that."

One of the boys said, "He did, Ty. He just got—"

"Rat it! Go ahead, Kiley. Make the point. I'm listening."

"I don't expect an answer to this now. I'm not really asking what your plans are. But I'll guess that you figure to cripple services here inside till Security's forced to shut down the field. That's what I might do, anyway, *if*—get this now—*if* I didn't know any better. Or, say, you're figuring a way to break out." Kiley searched the watching faces. He'd hit it. He could see in their tension. That was their plan.

"But . . . what can you *do* out there? The minute Washington hears that we've got trouble inside, they'll send troops. They've got the power. You'll never make it."

"Ty? Maybe—"

"No! Why listen? How do we know we can trust him? Remember this?" Tyrone ducked behind the table and came up waving a book.

"This was the last time he decided to *help*. You want more of the same?"

A low muttering spread through the crowded alcove.

It reassured rather than troubled Kiley. He had enough of them uncertain that he might yet begin to sway them. He spoke calmly, dispassionately, with measured logic. "Try this. Haller's quit. Did you know that? Fine. Here's what I'm suggesting. I'm putting my name in for president. If you—"

"Good rat, man! Is this a campaign speech?" Tricia asked. "If you try some more of that *election* cloudmouth on us—"

"Dammit! Just listen! Start it another way. If this place breaks down, Morgan's sure to contact Washington. All I'm suggesting is that I'm on your side. The best way I prove it is, you help elect me. I'll see that some changes are made. And right now! We'll spend a year at it. A year till Morgan goes back to Washington. Working together that whole time, we *can* get something done. We *can* get ready to shut down the field. But not overnight. Doesn't that make sense?"

"It makes garbage, Kiley," Tricia said. "We don't need—"

"No. Hold it." Tyrone cut her off. "Let's think about it."

"Ty? You're not serious?"

"I said 'think.' We can go that far. What do you want? You want to get free? Or you want to get free *our way*? What's that but pride?"

Kiley examined faces warily. He couldn't really tell which way they were leaning. But at least Tyrone was making sense. It was a beginning.

"All right, Kiley. We'll talk it over. Maybe you're right. But I can't decide that myself, not without more than your word. That's pretty cheap currency right now."

"I know. All I'm asking is some time. Help elect me. Let me prove what I'm saying." He stood drained. If that wouldn't persuade them at least to delay, he had nothing else to offer. He understood their hesitancy. He respected it. Why *should* they listen to him? He doubted that he would, in their place.

"We'll try it," Tyrone said.

"Rat shit!" Tricia snapped. She threw herself into her chair and sat glaring at them.

"I'm the man, true?"

"Hey."

"We'll try it. Give us a couple days. Say, next Monday. We'll let you know by then. 'sky?"

"Fair enough," Kiley said.

"You. Margaret. Take him out." Tyrone motioned a gangling black girl to him. "You know the way."

Only as they left the alcove did Kiley feel the tic twitching his cheek. He tried to relax as he followed the girl back through the maze. Convincing them wouldn't be easy. Not with two days left in which to prove himself. He had no idea how to do that.

50

TYRONE LAID a hand on Tricia's shoulder. She jerked away in anger.

"I mean it, Ty. Rat shit! I thought you had a head on you. And now this. You really think he's going to do us any good?"

"No. Not a lick."

Everyone stared in bewilderment.

"Then what are you—"

"Enough. Just listen. Maybe he can do one thing for us. If he's out there trying to keep the pressure off, won't that help?"

"So what? Two days won't be—"

"Just enough." Tyrone grinned. "For now, we're moving to Twenty-two duct, in case Kiley can find his way back here. Call the cell leaders in. They'll come fast enough. Tell them we're going outside. Tomorrow night."

"You mean it?"

"So soon?"

"What if—"

"Quiet! Let Kiley make his plans. Before he knows what we're doing, we'll be gone. Warren? Want to tell them?"

The small boy hopped off the box he had been sitting on. "I talked to Fat Ethel. Did you know she's my mother? Well, *she* knows. I think maybe Ty's got it figured."

Willis stepped forward. "Kiley could be right—"

The others drowned him out with their shouting. Tricia threw herself at Tyrone and wrestled him to the floor in her happiness, while the others gathered closer and laughed excitedly.

51

"At least they haven't knocked out the phones," Jackie greeted him. "Six calls since you left—Bengston, Clausewitz, even Morgan phoned."

"About what?" Kiley flopped into a chair and tried to sort fact from fancy in his recollection of the interview with Tyrone. Two days. He had somehow to persuade the students not to risk repression worse than what they now endured, and at the same time prove that he intended to help them.

Jackie sat silent until Kiley's glazed eyes focused on her. "You okay now? Want to tell me what they said?"

"In a minute. What were the calls?"

"Who can tell? Half panic, half politics. Bengston wouldn't come right out and say it, but I got the impression he'd support you if you ran for president."

"Perfect. That could do it. Can you get him for me?" Pieces began to fall into place. Kiley considered himself a clumsy politician, but skilled enough to accept the rising tide of pressure behind his candidacy. Then, riding before that wave, he'd be free to change directions as circumstances dictated. Haller had lacked any power. But Kiley wasn't Haller, and there was a new Morgan to deal with.

"He's on," Jackie whispered. She sidled out of phone view and nodded toward the screen.

"Bob? Good to see you again. How was the trip?" Bengston wore new bags under his eyes. He looked harried, his close-cropped silver hair a nest of matted cowlicks.

"You didn't call me about that, did you?"

"Well. To be perfectly frank, I wanted to thank you." Bengston shook a playful finger. "Had me worried there, you did. Morgan tells me the budget hearings worked out fine. I should have known you'd support us, Bob-oh. Some of my colleagues weren't certain about you, but I said all along, 'If Doctor Bengston knows people, and I feel he does, Bob Kiley is one of us.' Was it the Stimucenter? What convinced you—"

"Howie? Can we talk about the latest confusion?"

Bengston slumped with relief. "Then you know. Those goddamned kids! Just when everything was working out, then they take it into their heads to foul up—"

"What are we going to do about it?" Kiley interrupted.

"Do? How the hell. . . . 'We'? What should we do? Well now, Bob-oh. As long as you put it that way, I did have an idea. Have you heard? Haller's resigned, and some of us here feel you might be just the man to replace him."

"Me? As president? Not a chance!" Kiley frowned slightly in answer to Jackie's surprised look. He shook his head. And waited.

In something less than four minutes of earnest pleading, Bengston persuaded him. Through it all Kiley felt more and more the hypocrite, particularly at having to ignore Jackie's delight and appear somber as he let himself be talked into his own intention. The whole process was tedious, but necessary.

Agreeing reluctantly, he sprung his trap. "Maybe you're right, Howie. *But.* There's only one way I'd even consider it. I want a promise. If I accept, I have a free hand in disciplining the students."

"Absolutely! Of course. Hang the sonsabitches. What do I care?

Do you know they shorted out almost every one of our classrooms? The little bastards deserve whatever they get. We can't run a class without—"

"Howie? Hold it. When I said 'disciplining,' I had something particular in mind."

"Oh?" Bengston turned to look at someone offscreen. He shrugged, then focused again on Kiley. "Fine. Whatever you say, Bob. Get this mess straightened out, that's all we care about."

"Don't agree so quickly. If I'm elected, the first thing I'll expect is a joint Bizad-Fac declaration of amnesty for all the rebels."

"Amnesty! After what they've done? You can't just let it go. A bunch of addicts like that? They'll run crazy! No. I feel—"

"Sorry, then. But thanks for thinking of me." Kiley reached for the phone switch, in calculated slow motion. He fought the smile Bengston's sudden desperation inspired.

"Hey! Hold on!" Bengston raised both hands in surrender. "Now wait, Bob. Wait a minute. If that's the only way . . . if you. . . ." He took a deep breath. "Fine. Whatever you say. All we ask is, get them to calm down. Can you do that?"

"I can try. One more thing. Some Fac might not be too happy to know who asked me to run for this office. Do you see what I—"

"Of course. Certainly, my boy. It's our little secret. Not a word to anyone."

"I'll run as an independent."

Bengston winked. "Our secret. Would you like us to put up a token opposition? We could—"

"Howie? Let it go. Just get your students to vote for me. Nothing else. Let me handle the rest of it."

"Certainly. Anything you say, Bob-oh. And when it's all over, you'll have to come to dinner." Bengston leaned forward in conspiracy. "I have a friend you might like to meet, if you and that Muller woman. . . . Well, you know." His hands sketched an hourglass in the air.

"Thank you, Howie. I'll think about it." He flipped the switch.

"*Will* you think about it?" Jackie asked.

"Not now. Not if you can get Clausewitz on the phone."

Kiley went through the same contrived reluctance. He let himself be persuaded to run for the presidency on two conditions: that Fac not openly support him; that he have a guarantee of amnesty for the rebels. Clausewitz opposed both conditions. He also agreed to both conditions.

After two hours on the phone, Kiley had amassed all the good will he thought he could use: Hobart Reid; Trotter; J. Cameron Rudnick, who promised media support; Haller, and Haller's public endorsement. Everyone he could think of. Only one fact left him less than certain of the election's outcome. None of the people who promised support could vote. Only students, and only students under twenty-one at that, had the ballot. Though Fac and Bizads could pressure the nonrebels among their students, no one knew how Tyrone's forces might vote.

"If I understand them at all," he told Jackie, "they won't oppose. They may 'vote' by staying away from the polls. Even that will be enough."

"Will being president matter that much?"

"Not unless I can negate Morgan's power. That's next. In fact, this whole election is a fraud. I'm depending on Clausewitz to wander around complaining about the amnesty he had to guarantee. If Tyrone and the others hear that, they may believe me."

"I believe you."

"You're prejudiced. Now. Let's have something to eat, and relax. Those wheels grind exceeding slow. All we can do is wait."

Hands clasped behind his neck, he leaned back to enjoy the feeling the past hours had earned him. Accepting credit for *The Kiley Proposal* hadn't been nearly so satisfying as this. He was finally involved. Intentionally. His own way. Not merely fronting for others. Uncertainties nagged at him. He couldn't know that, even given a full year in which to remold the university, he could tear down the forcefield. But he would be in a position to try, and that was a beginning. Whatever ensued, good or ill, would be in a large part up to him. Credit, or blame—he could accept either one. Someone had to.

He rummaged through a nightstand drawer and found a pencil and paper. Another of his old habits returned to him. He would make a list. In black and white, his options would be easier to evaluate.

It was dark outside before he had jotted down more than a dozen possibilities. He wrote with one hand, ate with the other, occasionally asking Jackie's advice or opinion. A program developed before his eyes, under his own hand. He leaned back to examine the whole scheme.

A single phone call destroyed it.

"Mis' Kiley? 'member me?" It was "Willis," the boy who had interrupted Kiley's single class meeting. Though his head was shaved, he still wore the identifying glasses. "Tyrone an them's breakin out tomorrow night."

"What? What are you talking about? They said—"

"It's no time to 'splain. Tomorrow night. At Exit East. An doan forget who tole you."

"I still don't under—"

"We ain all like Tyrone. It's lots of us like what you done here. You won't forget, will you?" Willis hung up.

"What did he mean?" Jackie asked. "Who was that?"

"A weasel I know." He tore up his list and started over.

52

INSIDE THE MOUTH of Twenty-duct, the winding, windy tunnels were filled with children. They stood, backs against the wall, as far as Tyrone could see, even farther out of sight around the nearest bend. All dressed in gray warmth for "outside," nearly all the same height—with here and there a single figure rising tall above the uniformity of the rest—they lined the walls with colorlessness. Tyrone saw only a portion of the first contingent: nearly one hundred volunteers with enough confidence in his plan to risk leading the way to freedom. As soon as this vanguard reached safety outside, a few would dart back in to give the all-clear to others already massing behind them in alcoves, and byways, and every conceivable bend and twist of the tunnel system near Exit East.

Tyrone made a last check. "Set, Warren?"

"I talked to Fat Ethel—"

"Can't you say 'mother'?" Tricia interrupted.

"Mother, then. I talked to her like you said, and she understands. She'll let us through."

Tyrone squeezed Tricia's hand. "'sky. I *knew* it could work. No violence. No killings. Just a simple breakout and scatter."

None of the three voiced the fears they all felt. Some would be caught; some would be returned—to what, none of them knew.

"Most of us will make it, ain't so, Ty?"

He squeezed her hand again. "Pass it back. We're going."

Like a cresting wave breaking above gray waters, heads turned and passed the word in whispers.

Tyrone led the way out of the duct mouth into deepening twilight. "Outside," it was nearly night. "Inside," the filter of the force-field above turned the evening sky a gummy olive. The line of crouching children walked on eggs through the shadows.

The inner door to the exit chamber stood open, waiting, and Tyrone led them along the railroad tracks into the bright artificial light inside. Still they kept close to the wall and beneath the control room window. Ethel Pease had obviously cleared the way for them, but training dies hard. No one wanted to show himself. For all their bravado they were fearful and uncertain.

Ahead of them, at the end of the exit chamber, the outer door stood ajar. Beyond it the sky was a deep blue velvet invitation.

"Opensky!" Tricia hissed. It was half a prayer.

"Shhhh!"

They had nearly reached the outer door when a loudspeaker boomed, "Don't crawl. Go out on your feet."

Startled treble voices rose in clamor; two of the children bolted back the way they'd come.

"Freeze!" Tyrone shouted. "Hold it!"

Quiet settled over them.

They heard only their own hearts pounding.

Nothing happened.

Tyrone stepped to the center of the tracks and turned to look for the speaker. His chest constricted, and he blinked sweat out of his eyes. The air smelled strangely sweet here, near opensky, cloying and so unfamiliar that he caught a part of himself trying to identify the rare aroma. Freedom has its own scent.

Then he saw Kiley standing behind the observation window. "Yes. It's me."

Warily, Tyrone glanced at both open doors. A smaller portal, man-sized and beneath the window through which Kiley watched, was closed. No other Fac in sight; no trap that Tyrone could recognize. He tried to appear confident.

"I relieved Miss Pease, if that's what you're thinking. She's fine. Nothing will happen to her. But I have to ask if you're sure you want to do this."

Several of the children shook their heads. A few were close to tears; on other faces determined anger showed.

"Yes! We're sure!"

"No need to shout. There's a mike out there with you. Think a minute before you take that last step. If—"

"How did you know?" Tyrone demanded. Some sense told him that they were safe. He couldn't understand it all—it was happening too quickly—but he knew. They were free now, no matter what Kiley might say.

"That doesn't matter. This does. I came to help. You won't believe that you're making a mistake, but you have to believe I'm on your side, no matter what happens from here on."

Something in Kiley's tone frightened him again. It seemed a sadness, or awareness of inevitability. He refused to recognize the implications of Kiley's presence or to show his fears. Not in front of the others. "I doubt that!" he shouted, as if mere sound could drown out his thoughts. "Why are you here?"

"I *am* here. Do you see any guards? Any weapons? Think it over. Turn around now, all of you, and nothing will happen. Remember the election. Help me. Help me help *you*." Kiley's tongue felt like leather. He tried to find the magic phrase that might persuade them, but even as he stood and heard the echo of his words die away, he knew he was failing.

Desperately: "Please! You're a rational human being. Think, man! Use your head. You *know* I'm right. Come inside here with me. You and I. We can talk about it. Then, if you still want to leave, fine. But let's discuss it. What are a couple of minutes more?"

"Now!" Tricia shouted. "We go now!" She bolted for the patch of dark sky and the others followed in a shouting, jostling horde.

Tyrone held up a hand to stem the flow. The gesture was futile.

He smiled and walked after them. He had brought them this far, they were right to go on without him. Each one alone. He waved at Kiley. There was no animosity in it, no challenge. He didn't feel that he had won anything, or lost. He walked calmly, deliberately, while children dashed past him on both sides. Running, for him, would be wrong.

Kiley ached with disappointment. "I tried. I really tried."

Morgan stepped from the shadows behind him and peered down into the chamber. "And failed. Now, by Christ! You better be right about the rest of it, or it's on your head."

Kiley nodded wearily. "Send them out."

The small door beneath the window opened and a file of Security guards entered the exit chamber into view. Each wore a helmet and dark goggles; on each helmet was a miner's lamp. They carried stretchers, not weapons.

The children pouring through the chamber hesitated. A few hurled curses and sprinted on past. Most stopped at seeing the guards towering over them, then whirled to run back toward the duct mouth shouting, "It's a trap! Go back!" They collided with those behind them, fell over one another, clogging the chamber with bodies, and fought to escape. Escape—now—in both directions. Their panic spread. Blindly, heedlessly, they ran, driving the latecomers before them in their flight.

Soon the exit chamber was empty.

"Let's go," Morgan said.

Outside, Kiley counted twenty-seven of the students lying within fifty yards of the exit port. Most cowered on the winter-killed grass bordering the base of the forcefield. Several knelt with their heads buried in folded arms; a few were stretched prone and scratched feebly at the ground as if trying to burrow to safety. One girl lay flat on her back and stared up through the vast darkness at a panorama of stars gleaming brilliant white in the crisp night air. Her whole body shook with violent tremors.

"One of you get the doctor over here," Kiley said.

A guard knelt beside the girl.

The guards worked methodically. Protected by their dark goggles, they saw nothing but the puddled infrared circles cast by each helmet lamp. When a pool of sweeping light located one of the children, a guard would help him back toward a string of ambulances, which were filing into the exit chamber. None of the guards could see opensky. Each was safe in his personal blindness.

Beyond the fallen children a few of the stronger ones staggered uncertainly away. Gently, guards took each one by the arm and turned him back toward the university.

Tyrone stood with legs spread, head bent low, his eyes closed. He trembled but held himself erect by force of will, waiting. "Kiley? Are you there?" Cords on his neck stood out in bold relief. He held his hands clasped behind him. His fists were clenched, the nails drew blood.

"KILEY!"

"Here." Kiley touched his shoulder.

Tyrone jerked away and nearly fell. Still he held his eyes closed. "Oh, you, sonofabitch! You had the guards all ready. You rat-sucking urban! You're a dead man, Kiley."

Kiley motioned a guard near. "Keep your eyes shut," he told Tyrone. He nodded to the guard. "Take him inside."

Within twenty minutes, all the children had been helped, or carried, to the ambulances.

Morgan offered thanks. "I owe you for this. I wasn't sure you knew what you were doing. Is it settled now?"

"If you don't call Washington, no one else can."

"It's nothing to me," Morgan said. "I'm just here to keep the peace. As long as I don't hear about any trouble, there's no trouble. And, thanks again."

"No trouble," Kiley said.

Morgan didn't hear the irony in Kiley's voice.

53

"Individual personality enrichment or traffic in mere ideas—those aims contend for our approval. We can hardly doubt which will prevail."

Afterword, *The Kiley Proposal*

THE REBELLION was over in hours. By four in the morning, thirty-five ringleaders lay sedated in hospital rooms commandeered by Morgan. Many of the other stricken children still suffered mild disorientation but would recover in a day or so. Although the shock of facing opensky, unprepared, had been severe, it would have no permanent effect.

(Ask the behaviorists: rats raised in cubicles with electrified walls will lie cowering helplessly, even after the walls have been removed. For a time. Eventually, many of them will come to accept freedom as a natural state. Well, they may not accept it completely, but they will become fit for other experiments.)

A late winter's dawn showed its lime pallor within the university before Kiley got to bed. He had made a final check to make certain that the hospital staff understood his instructions (conveyed through

Morgan). As a gesture he will never completely understand himself, he asked that Tyrone Floy be given the hospital's newly named Kiley Room.

Though Tyrone had lost the battle, the war was not over. Kiley hoped.

He slept till noon.

Jackie woke him with the news. He was now the president of Urban University. And the phone calls had already begun.

He ignored them and ate a hearty meal.

"Are we moving to Haller's house?" Jackie asked.

"Not yet. First, I'll have to get hold of Clausewitz and Bengston, separately. We need the appearance of democracy, for a while at least. By tomorrow I want that declaration of amnesty, and it ought to seem their idea."

Jackie nodded. Her delight with the new order shone on her face. "We can turn the students loose."

"Not a chance," Kiley said. "They stay right where they are. Locked in. They can't give us any trouble where we can keep an eye on them."

"Bob! You don't mean that! After what you said?"

"Ignore what I said, or we'll be back where we started. Talk doesn't matter that much, not when we've got so many things to get done." He began to tick off items on his fingers. "First, let's make certain all the factories are back to capacity. If we fall down on orders, Washington will wonder. We have to keep them happy.

"Next, we can please Bizads and Fac by defining amnesty: ten months' imprisonment for the thirty-five in the hospital, freedom of the streets for all the rest."

"But what kind of amnesty—"

"Keep track. See what I overlook. Those thirty-five are the leaders. We'll assume they're the brightest, and therefore the most difficult to deal with. After we've checked through Fac records and located instructors, all the prisoners will begin rehabilitation. Eight hours a day, classes in American history, math, physics, and . . . well, we'll think of what else they need."

Shaking imaginary cobwebs out of her eyes, Jackie peered at him. "I think you're serious!"

"Saturday afternoons, we'll dilate the forcefield shell over University Park, whether it's raining or not. That'll do for the first month. Then we'll extend it to all day Saturday, and slowly increase the time. And remind me, will you? Any student who fails to make muster in the park when the field's open gets forbidden to attend reading classes for a week."

"Now I *know* you're not thinking. You mean *must* attend."

"No. Forbidden's the word. Why let them think it's punishment to go to class?"

"But, reading? They'll hate you!"

"Very likely. Then, for the thirty-five—"

"What if they don't want to?"

Kiley grinned. "Oh, they won't. Why should they? It will be hard work. But they'll do it."

Flustered, Jackie stammered through a list of unintelligible objections.

Kiley ignored her and poured another cup of coffee. "Now, I'll cook up a story to give Morgan. I'll explain it to him. As long as we can keep Washington in the dark, he won't care—"

"You haven't explained it to *me!*" she complained. "You know what you sound like? You're talking the worst kind of paternalism. Tyrone and them—uh, those others. Why should they bother with what *you* want them to learn?"

His grin faded. He fixed her with a stare. "Because I know what's best for them. Now, before you blow up, consider the rest of this rat's nest. What was Retardo all about? Your friends excuse their idiocy by claiming to give these kids what they want, right? But to guarantee that students won't want anything too threatening, or too demanding for mindless nits like Clausewitz, it's safest to see them as children. Children are easy to satisfy. Give them candy. For every meal. You can go along with that if you like, but I won't. I don't believe it for a minute. Candy isn't love, it isn't even respect. So now, we'll do it my way. Because—I know what's best for them."

For a long moment she was literally speechless. "All on your say-so?"

"Dammit, Jackie! Isn't that what's going on now?"

"No. We both know better than that. They may *think* you and those books are the same thing—"

He interrupted to finish her sentence: "'But we know better.' Well, that's what I'm saying. We know better. The defense rests."

Jackie was torn. She agreed, and didn't enjoy agreeing, not after the lifetime of impulses that had drawn her to the university in the first place. Yet the only objection she could offer sounded feeble to her own ears. "The students will hate you."

"At first. But Tyrone will come around. He's too bright not to understand. Besides, they don't have to love me. They only have to do what I tell them."

"You could be *wrong!*"

His smile returned. "'Could be'? I'd say the odds are ten to one I *will* be, but consider something: can I be more wrong than before? Remember, I've been out there. They haven't. Someone has to let them know about it, unless you still think it's a favor to keep them so incompetent that they have to stay in this place."

This place, he understood in the midst of his own comment, was Kiley House, on Kiley Avenue, and no one living really belonged in it or near it. He will not tear it down, although his impulses suggest that step; it will serve as a focal point for the dislike all students will feel for him.

"Here's something else," he added. "Tyrone, half his friends, they've already learned to read. On their own. Because they need it."

"Ahhhhh, see! *They* wanted to. But they don't want the rest of that list you named. Next thing you'll be claiming they ought to study biology, or French, or . . . or poetry!" Her imagination reached its limits.

"No. We'll be lucky to find anyone who can explain elementary physics to them. I'm sure there's not a biologist left. . . . Wait a minute. Morgan can *get* one!"

Unconvinced, Jackie surrendered. She took his cup of cold coffee and muttered, "I know they'll hate you for it."

He laid a hand on hers. "Then they won't hate their instructors. Let me be the villain, if that's what it takes. And remind me, will you? I want to see whether Wallace, that bodyguard, is still around."

"Do you think they'll do anything?" She rose in concern and looked over her shoulder. "They *killed* Borgward when he was president. If—"

"Hey. Easy now. *Someone* killed Borgward. That's all we know. And you can be sure I'm not looking for martyrdom.

"Tomorrow, you and I start working with the thirty-five in the hospital. They'll make a cadre; the others will listen to them. We've got a year, if we can keep Morgan in line. And at the very least, we've got a couple of months before anyone really starts getting upset by the minor changes—"

At that instant, the first stone will come crashing through the window. It showers glass over the table and floor.

Kiley will drag Jackie under the table and lie awkwardly waiting for a second missile.

Outside Kiley House, on Kiley Avenue, near the campus center of Urban University, a student whose name we don't know, one whom Kiley will have nicknamed "Willis," will be unable to find another stone.

Not then.

Not at that moment.